# SHOCKWAVE

## Praise for the Jack Courtney Adventures

'An exciting and realistic story, full of bandits, poachers and amazing wildlife . . . it keeps you turning the pages to the end' – *i* newspaper

'Unputdownable . . . Fast-moving adventure with heart and a message . . . Jack is as appealing a hero as Anthony Horowitz's Alex Rider' – LoveReading4Kids

'You won't be able to put it down' – Angels & Urchins

'Filled with so many twists and turns it will keep the reader guessing . . . Fans of Enid Blyton and Willard Price will enjoy *Cloudburst*, which takes these classics, injecting them with a modern influence' – Reading Zone

'An exciting and powerful story brimming with fast-paced action, unexpected twists and turns, an extraordinary backdrop and a cast of inspirational characters' – Pam Norfolk

'The Democratic Republic of Congo provides a colourful and vibrant backdrop f       exciting new
childrer                                              reFly

# THE JACK COURTNEY ADVENTURES

*Cloudburst*
*Thunderbolt*
*Shockwave*

# WILBUR SMITH

## WITH CHRIS WAKLING

# SHOCKWAVE

First published in Great Britain in 2022 by
PICCADILLY PRESS
4th Floor, Victoria House, Bloomsbury Square
London WC1B 4DA
Owned by Bonnier Books, Sveavägen 56, Stockholm, Sweden
www.piccadillypress.co.uk

A CIP catalogue record for this book is available from the British Library.

ISBN: 978-1-84812-857-6
*Also available as an ebook and in audio*

1

This book is typeset using Atomik ePublisher
Printed and bound in Great Britain by Clays Ltd, Elcograf S.p.A.

Piccadilly Press is an imprint of Bonnier Books UK
www.bonnierbooks.co.uk

*For all our young readers and their families*
*Wilbur Smith & Chris Wakling*

# 1.

The snow crust broke before I'd even cut my first turn down the slope. More fissures immediately shot out from the first. As I saw the whiteness around me shatter, I heard the electric crackling of the snow slab breaking up.

I'd triggered an avalanche.

It looked beautiful: like a spider's web spreading out down the mountainside. But the cascading snow was behind me as well as in front of me, and although I tried to ski across it – that's what our instructor Sylvan had told us to do if we found ourselves in this *très grave* situation – the white wave immediately engulfed me.

I was upended. The snow ripped my skis from their bindings. I was swept away.

Sylvan had also told us to jettison our ski poles if an avalanche struck. So, as I was rag-dolling my way down the slope, blinded, carried by the roaring snow, that's what I tried to do. The pole straps were looped around my wrists. I somehow managed to shake one free. It took a ski glove with it. But I couldn't get the other pole off. It spun with me as I cartwheeled down the mountain.

How could this be happening?

We'd been so careful. I'd studied the forecast, read the snow, checked everything.

It didn't matter. The avalanche was in charge now.

Where was Amelia? She'd dropped onto the slope ahead of me. Would she have had time to veer out of the path of the thundering wall of snow? You can't outrun an avalanche. Just like with a rip current in the sea, your best bet is to go at right angles to it and hope you can reach its edge. At least Xander was safe on his outcrop of rock. I didn't know which way was up. It was like being mashed up on the beach by a surf wave, but much, much worse.

As I was punched forward, I had time to think that Xander, piloting the drone, would be filming the whole thing from above, just as the GoPro on my helmet was capturing every millisecond of what I could – or couldn't – see.

We were in the Alps to make a film for a project called On the Brink. It was one of Mum's eco-initiatives. She'd taken a bit of convincing that epic shots of us carving fresh Alpine powder fitted with On the Brink's save-the-planet ethos, but I'd eventually managed to persuade her that showcasing some of the world's most beautiful – and threatened – landscape with a bit of extreme sports action, rather than just showing another scrawny polar bear on a melting ice floe, would add an unexpected angle.

Also, since we were young, any halfway-decent film we made for the cause might generate a bit of publicity. This wasn't exactly the footage I'd planned on capturing, but as long as I survived it would make for interesting viewing.

What else had Sylvan told us about avalanches? First, get the right gear. That included transceivers, extendable probes and snow shovels. Also, inflatable backpacks. We had all of that.

Second, learn how to work the gear. He'd demonstrated how to use the backpack on solid ground. I was still somersaulting inside the snow wave, but I knew what to do and managed to grab the toggle on my shoulder with my free hand.

Instantly the top of the pack blew itself up into an air-filled pillow. This was supposed to lift me up through the moving snow, so that when the avalanche finally came to a halt I'd be at the surface. Sylvan had also told us to try to 'swim' upwards. That was easier said than done; I still had no idea which way was up. I thrashed about instinctively anyway, and I took another piece of his advice while I was at it: holding my breath so as not to fill my lungs with powdered snow.

The avalanche couldn't have lasted more than thirty seconds, but it seemed to go on for hours, days, weeks. I tumbled along with it, lungs burning, arms and legs and head yanked this way and that, hoping against hope that I wouldn't hit a rock or tree. A quarter of all avalanche victims are killed that way. Most of the others who die suffocate when the snow stops. Would the backpack save me from that? The chaos ripped off my ski goggles. Finally, the frothing snow slowed down. I saw brightness above me.

It was full of white mist at first, but as I came to a stop and craned my neck, I glimpsed blue.

The sky! I'd never been so pleased to see it.

Why was it so difficult to move though? My arm with the ski pole attached to it was wedged behind me, and my legs felt as if they were set in cement. I tried rocking my body forwards and backwards to free myself, but the snow, full of air and energy one minute, had instantly solidified when the avalanche stopped. I could move one arm at least, so I tried to gouge away the snow and dig myself free with gloveless fingers.

What was that impatient buzzing? It took me a second to recognise the noise. I couldn't see far enough behind me to spot it, but it had to be Xander's drone. With his eye in the sky he'd surely spot me quickly and come to help dig me free.

But just as I deciphered it, the buzzing was drowned out by more rumbling, which made no sense at all. The avalanche was over. I'd come to a halt. All I had to do was free myself and make sure that Amelia was safe. Hopefully she'd pulled her own airbag toggle, or been able to avoid the whole thing.

The rumbling swelled to a roar. I turned my head to look back up the slope. What I saw simply couldn't be true. I was still wedged tight, unable to get up, let alone run away, from a *second* wave of snow that was racing towards me. Sylvan had said nothing about this! But it can happen: one slab of fresh snow breaks from the slope and disturbs another, which follows it down. I'd survived the first onslaught, but

I was encased in snow, powerless to escape the billowing second wave.

It really did look like white water tumbling over itself as it roared down the mountain, terrifyingly beautiful. I used the last piece of advice I could remember before the snow reached me, and tried to hold my arm in front of my face to create an air pocket. The roar of the second wave was jet-engine loud. It ran straight over me, a great obliterating wedge of whiteness, burying me alive.

## 2.

The noise and movement completely disorientated me. Had the second avalanche tumbled me further down the mountain? I didn't know. When the snow stopped, I wasn't sure which way was up. At least I still had my arm in front of my face. I managed to work it forward and back, enlarging the pathetically small hole it had preserved, but only a little. I blinked the snow from my eyes. Everything was ice blue.

I breathed out, then in.

Gravity, my enemy when the snow had been tumbling me down the mountain, was now my friend. I let a trickle of spit dribble out of my mouth. It slid down my chin. I hadn't been turned over, then: that way was still down and my hand was still pointing up.

How much snow was above me? Ten centimetres? A metre? Two? I worked my fingers into the roof of the hole, punch-jabbing at it, trying to break through, but I couldn't. Above me was just more snow. I was pinned in a straitjacket of the stuff, clamped tight from all sides. Panic bubbled up inside me.

'Help!' I shouted. 'Help!'

Though I bellowed with all my might, I could barely hear myself; I may as well have been yelling into a pillow wrapped in a duvet. My heart galloped in my ears. This wasn't good.

I fought to stay calm. They would be searching for me. The avalanche transceiver attached to my jacket would be pinging out its signal. And Xander had the drone footage. He and Amelia – I had to believe that she had escaped the avalanche and wasn't also trapped in it – would look back over the film to establish a good last-seen point. That's the first step in locating an avalanche victim. Then they'd use their own transceivers to listen out for the signal from mine, and come to find me.

Sylvan's instructions had been clear: searchers should sweep the debris field in quick zigzags until they pick up a signal. Once they've locked on, the next step is to slow down, pay close attention to the distance readings and directional lights on the transceiver, and pinpoint the casualty.

At two metres the directional lights turn off and the transceiver simply indicates distance. You have to look to find the lowest number – or burial depth, as it's known. Once you're certain the casualty is as near as dammit beneath you, you assemble your pole and start probing.

We'd practised that. You probe perpendicular to the slope in concentric circles until you have a positive strike. A body feels squishy but firm, Sylvan had said. We'd practised because knowing what to do could save a life. I'd memorised the whole drill. I'd just never seriously considered that the squishy-but-firm body in question might be mine.

The heat of my breath was melting the snow in front of my face, making droplets that instantly froze again. I tried to sip at the air, forced myself to breathe slowly, eke out the oxygen in my air pocket for as long as possible. Avalanche victims have about fifteen minutes before they suffocate. How long had I been buried? A minute? Five? Ten? What if they didn't get to me in time? I couldn't . . . wouldn't . . . mustn't die like this!

I thought of Mum. She'd lost my brother Mark in an accident I'd caused. And because of me she'd lost her husband, the man I'd called Dad, who I'd exposed as a corrupt villain, prepared to sacrifice us both for his own gain.

Her last words to me this morning had been 'Stay safe'.

And now look at me.

I'd taken Sylvan's briefings seriously. I'd tried to implement them. But I'd failed. I'd misread the snow, triggered the avalanche and got myself buried in it. I knew Mum was a strong woman, but if I died here, I'd be leaving her on her own.

Though I knew it would only make things worse, I couldn't stop myself from struggling in the snow, yelling for help, wasting energy and oxygen.

When I stopped, exhausted, a blackness descended. I felt cold, lost, ridiculous. They hadn't found me. Perhaps my transceiver was broken, or the drone had lost sight of me. Maybe Amelia was buried too. Hopefully Xander was digging her out. He wouldn't have time to find us both.

Another wave of loss – or a sense of unfinished business – crashed over me. I still had so much to do! Mostly I wanted to resolve things with the Leopard – the man Mum claimed was my real father, but who I'd seen buying child soldiers in Somalia. They both insisted he'd been trying to save them. The guy had written to me, asking to meet. I had blanked him. Why? To protect myself. Instinctively, I distrusted the guy: though I was intrigued by him, something about him made me wary. How stupid was that? I decided there and then that, if I got out of the snow alive, I'd find out exactly who the Leopard – or Jonny Armfield, to give him his actual name – really was.

That's all I had in those moments: a resolution rattling around my head. The snow had snuffed out everything else. I shut my eyes against the blue light and did the only thing I could: hung on in there. It didn't matter that everything ached, that my lungs hurt, that I was alone, trapped, cold, dying. I wasn't dead *yet*.

# 3.

Just as I was about to give up hope, something jabbed my thigh. I yelled Xander's name, but my voice was weak. For long seconds the probe didn't find me again. I began to doubt myself: had I imagined the sensation by wanting it so badly? No! The second time he poked me, he caught me in the side, quite hard.

I yelped, louder this time.

Squidgy but firm, I thought.

'Xander!' I shouted as loudly as I could.

This time I heard a muffled reply. Then the probe pierced the snow right next to my head. Quick as a flash, I grabbed the probe-tip with my free hand – partly to stop him taking out one of my eyes with his next stab, but mostly so I could hang on to it and let him know where to dig. He tugged; I tugged back. I'd thought I might die. Now I was being reborn. My hand was almost as blue-white as the snow in front of my face, but my grip on the probe was vice-like: nobody was about to tear that pole away from me.

Xander would be digging down the slope beneath me. Sylvan had explained: once you've located the casualty with your probe you dig a metre downhill from them, clearing the snow to the sides. The digging is usually the part that takes the longest, particularly if the casualty is buried deep. I waggled the probe above me, trying to create an air hole I could breathe through while Xander worked. I called out to him again. 'Is Amelia OK?'

The muffled reply came from not Xander but Amelia herself. 'Of course! I'm fine! You are too now. Unless you're hurt. Are you hurt?'

The relief I felt on hearing her voice was almost unbearable. 'I'm fine,' I yelled. 'Fine!'

'That's an overstatement,' she shouted back at me. 'But whatever.'

'Sit tight,' said Xander. 'We'll get you out of there.'

I knew it was a joke, but Amelia took the bait all the same. 'Sit tight? He's hardly going anywhere.'

She was right. I was buried under one and a half metres of tumbled snow. It took them quite a while to shift it. By the time Amelia and Xander had dug enough away to pull me free, a French mountain rescue team – called by Xander – had joined them. The cold had evidently got to me. I was beyond shivering. All I could think – or talk – about were my lost skis and missing pole. I wanted everyone to search for them, and even tried to set off and look myself, but the rescue team were having none of it. They wrapped me in two space blankets and loaded me onto their blood-wagon instead. I'd seen these bright red stretchers-on-skis before, but not up close. It was surprisingly snug and comfortable. I felt like I might fall asleep in it. In fact, I drifted off, only to be rudely awakened by a poke in the arm.

'Keep your eyes open!' Amelia told me. To Xander she said, 'He's hypothermic. It affects judgement first. Sufferers often spout nonsense. Then they fall asleep. Severe cases die.'

The ski-rescue guy evidently spoke good English. He stared at Amelia then said to me, 'She's a friend of yours, yes?'

I nodded.

Xander grinned. 'She means well. She just has a habit of telling it as it is.'

The ski-rescue guy shrugged and said, 'Nobody's dying.'

'Obviously,' replied Amelia. 'Foil blankets are highly efficient. He'll warm up again soon.' To me she added, 'But stay awake. Concentrate.'

Once the rescue team had strapped me in, they skied me across to the nearest piste and all the way down to the resort. It was the weirdest sensation to skim down the mountain on my back, watching the clouds and trees slide by above me, with Xander and Amelia skiing alongside as the two-man mountain rescue crew, one at my head and one at my feet, made easy work of the slopes.

By the time we'd made it back to town I was already feeling a bit better, but they weren't about to set me free. Instead they took me to the local medical centre, where a kind nurse gave me a mug of hot onion soup. After a long wait, during which I slowly warmed up, a doctor with a ginger beard examined me from head to toe. I was fine, and kept telling him so, but all he said in reply was, 'I'll be the judge. Wait here.' Then he left me in the consultation room.

I wasn't alone for long. Amelia and Xander soon came in. Xander had already begun cutting his drone film with the footage I'd taken on my helmet-cam and, while we waited, we watched it back on his phone.

The film showed me spearing down a slope that gave way as I went, the snow slab detonating and sliding and rushing to engulf me, while Amelia, still in shot, jinked left through a stand of firs, shooting to safety with – I have to admit it – superb skill. The drone then zoomed in on me, a slam-dunked doll, smacked left and right by tumbling chunks of snow until the powder, surging like white water, overtook everything. I was just visible after the first rush of snow stopped, but the second rubbed me out completely. Although I knew I'd survived, the footage of the avalanche burying me was hard to watch.

Xander – quick-thinking as always – kept the drone hovering above the spot where I'd disappeared. The film showed Amelia and Xander zigzagging towards me. Cut through it were snatches of the view through my helmet-cam. Once I'd been buried, all it filmed was the awful blueness of the snow, but it had been recording sound as well as visuals. I'd shouted for help more times than I realised.

And help had come. The drone footage showed Amelia and Xander methodically sweeping the broken snow-slope, searching and stopping and probing and shovelling, a picture of focused activity. I sat in the medical centre and watched my friends dig me from the brink of death. They'd been my back-up when I needed it most, and I knew, if I asked, they'd back me up with Jonny Armfield – the Leopard – too. Was he for real, or was he a threat? With their help, I'd find out.

# 4.

When Mum turned up at the medical centre, she hugged me so hard that it hurt. She thanked the ginger-bearded doctor profusely and he finally declared me fit to go. I could tell she didn't know how to feel: furious at me for getting myself caught in an avalanche, or relieved that I was OK. Her response was to call Sylvan and arrange to meet him that evening.

Did she intend to blame him somehow? I had to head that off.

'It wasn't his fault,' I said as we waited in the chalet lobby. 'He briefed us well. I must have missed something. Without his instructions, Xander and Amelia wouldn't have got to me so fast, if at all. You have to remember that.'

'I just want him to see the footage,' she replied.

Sylvan arrived, wearing jeans and a thick knitted jumper. I'd only ever seen him in ski gear before. Without his ski goggles on, the tan-line across his sharp cheeks made him looked panda-eyed. He peered at Xander's film, right through to the end, biting his lower lip all the while. When it had finished, he puffed out his cheeks. Then he scrolled back to the start and tapped forward, pretty much frame by frame, scrutinising the intercut drone and helmet-cam footage we had recorded before committing to the slope. I waited for his verdict. What danger sign had I missed?

'It was fresh powder, but not too much, and the slope looks steep.'

'Way steeper than the 30–45 degrees you warned us about,' I said.

'Yes, more sluff than slab avalanche territory, and there's been no rapid temperature change. Also, you had tree cover to one side.'

'It wasn't a gully,' I said. 'No cornices or pillows . . . that I could see, at least.'

'No.' Sylvan sat back and ran a hand through his black curls. 'And yet, avalanche. It can happen. Very bad luck.'

'You're not wrong there,' said Amelia.

I realised that I'd been hunched over waiting for his opinion, and squared my shoulders now that he had delivered it.

'That was some nice skiing you did to get out of the way,' Sylvan said to Amelia.

She shrugged. 'Instinct, plus technique.'

'Textbook search-and-dig. Most impressive from the pair of you. And you, Jack, you deployed the inflatable backpack promptly. If not, you could have been buried deeper still.'

I didn't like to think about that.

Sylvan nodded at Xander. 'You also got what you came for. If at a cost.'

Xander looked confused.

'Dramatic film for the competition thing.'

'Ha. I suppose so.'

'A silver lining.' Sylvan patted me on the shoulder. 'You're a fortunate guy to have got away with it.'

'That doesn't quite stack up with the "very bad luck" you just mentioned,' said Amelia, 'but I know what you mean, I suppose.'

There were only a couple more days of the trip left. Although I did ski, I had no appetite for going off-piste. We took it easy, stuck to mostly red runs with the occasional black to keep things interesting. On our last evening, after eating more cheese fondue than you'd think possible, I slumped down on the reindeer-skin covered armchair in the chalet's pine-panelled lounge and said, 'I've got something on my mind,' to the only other people there, Amelia and Xander.

'I've never understood that expression,' said Amelia. 'Why isn't it something *in* my mind?'

Xander ignored her. 'What is it?'

'You remember that dodgy Leopard guy in Somalia?'

'Er, yeah,' Xander replied.

Amelia rolled her eyes. It had been a stupid question; the man had saved us from a band of child soldiers run by a psychopath called General Sir, though he'd apparently done his share of business with the General before that. None of us would ever forget him.

'Well, his real name is Jonny Armfield, and I want to find out more about him,' I said.

My friends exchanged a knowing look. Amelia said, 'Yeah, we wondered if you might.'

I think to steer me away from wondering why they'd been talking about me behind my back, Xander said, 'I want to get to the bottom of what he was doing out there too, for Mo's sake.'

Mo was the Somali boy pirate and solider without whose help we'd still probably have been hostages, or dead. Though Mo had subsequently managed to escape the camp himself, Armfield had apparently been prepared to let him rot there.

'In fact, we've already begun digging,' Amelia said.

'Just a bit of online research,' said Xander. 'Nothing too involved.'

I knew this wouldn't be true. Amelia doesn't do anything by halves, and Xander prides himself on keeping a step or two ahead of everybody else on tech stuff. I let my silence speak for me and eventually he went on, as I knew he would.

'Armfield doesn't exactly do social media. And his name doesn't crop up on any government or corporate websites.'

'You've tried all the aliases?'

'Leopold, Leopard, et cetera,' said Xander. 'And every variant.'

'Plus his real name,' Amelia added. 'Nothing comes up.'

A log shifted in the open fire, sending sparks up the chimney, bright against the blackened brickwork. Again, I kept quiet, leaving a gap one of them would sooner or later fill.

'But there's a web behind the web, isn't there?' Xander said.

'For the unsavoury and untrustworthy,' Amelia added.

Xander shrugged. 'If you know where to look, the dark web exists. And I've made a bit of progress there. Not much, though it's a lead.'

This time I couldn't hold back. 'A lead pointing which way?'

# 5.

Xander fired up his laptop to show me what he'd found out. The first website he clicked on was for an outfit called GreenSword Investments. It was about as boring as it sounds. A cursory look through the 'Mission Statement' and 'About Us' pages revealed that the company did what its name suggested. It invested money. What it invested in was all a bit vague, but the gist of it seemed to be energy projects. The good sort that generate power responsibly from renewable sources. They were keen to emphasise that.

There were lots of stock photographs of wind turbines and dams, and headshots of smiling men and women in suits and high-vis and hard hats, and the text accompanying them was all about commitment to sustainability and protecting the environment while delivering blah blah blah. Mum would have approved. There didn't seem to be much detail about which projects the company had invested in, but the web designer had used a fair few photos of rainforests and icebergs to give a general sense of what was important to GreenSword.

'OK,' I said. 'But what's this got to do with Armfield? I don't see him anywhere.'

'No,' said Xander. 'But the reason I looked up the company at all was because his name came up in an encrypted chain of messages I unearthed.'

I knew Xander wouldn't explain what 'unearthed' had entailed. He's too modest for that. I checked his face and, sure enough, it was as deadpan as ever, his expression showing neither pride nor need of praise.

'Yeah, he's been in touch with these guys. I haven't been able to dig back to who contacted who first, but it seems he's recently agreed to act as some sort of consultant for them.'

'How do you know it's him?'

Xander turned to me. 'There's such a thing as a digital footprint. If you hook into it, until the target gets wise you can follow pretty much every virtual trail they go down. Whoever I was following trashed their links just after I locked on. Could have been a routine clear-out, or they might have deliberately blocked me. Either way, I think I'm on to something.'

'Can you get another hook into him?'

'I'll keep trying, but the trail has gone cold for now.'

'What else have you been able to find out about this GreenSword outfit?' asked Amelia.

'Not much. The website is pretty new. As far as I can see, they haven't been mentioned on social media.'

'That's odd,' said Amelia. 'You'd think a new business would want to announce its arrival.'

'Not necessarily.' Xander shrugged. 'It looks to be a privately backed investment fund. They're not trying to raise money; they're just on the hunt for good ways of spending it. I'm sure they'll publicise the deals they do when they do them.'

That sounded reasonable. The screen lit Xander's even features with a bluish tint, at odds with the warm glow of the fire. I got up and added a log to the flames, collapsing the husk of ash beneath it. 'What do the emails say, exactly? Is there any detail about what sort of "consulting" he's agreeing to do for them?'

'Not much. They mention "reconnaissance" and "security", though what or who he's supposed be investigating or protecting is a mystery.'

'For now, you said,' said Amelia.

Xander smiled. 'Yeah, I'm working on it.'

Mum came into the room as Xander said this, and asked, 'Working on what?'

Xander didn't reply, but Amelia instinctively drew breath to explain. Luckily, she caught my eye and saw me imperceptibly shake my head. I surprised myself doing that. In general, I don't keep secrets from Mum. But for some reason I didn't want her to know that I was interested in this Armfield guy. She had wanted me to meet him after he'd helped to end our nightmare in Somalia, but I'd refused. She'd been hoodwinked by the man I called 'Dad' but she clearly trusted this Armfield bloke; it had hurt her when I wouldn't meet

22

with him. I didn't want to get her hopes up until I was sure he was legit.

'The film,' said Xander smoothly. 'Although it's not quite the On the Brink angle we'd hoped for, it's undeniably dramatic. I'm going to edit it properly and we're going to submit it to the competition anyway. It's worth a shot.'

Though I didn't like him lying to her, what he said was partly true. We had talked about producing a proper edit of the film. Since I was still kneeling beside the fire, I prodded a swarm of sparks from it with the poker. They disappeared up the chimney, taking my guilt with them: at least I hadn't lied to her myself, I suppose.

# 6.

As it happened, it was Amelia who found out more about GreenSword Investments ahead of Xander, and not by snooping online. She read it in a newspaper. The *Financial Times*, no less. She wasn't even looking specifically; she speed-reads that most boring of papers – as well as most of the other broadsheets – in her local library all the time, and has done since she was about eight. Less than a week after we got back to England, she came upon a short article mentioning the new company, buried among the other stultifying business news on the paper's pink pages.

We were in my kitchen drinking banana and blueberry smoothies when she told us this news. Mum was out, so I'd not washed the blender or binned the banana skins yet. The mess was spread between us on the kitchen island we were sitting at.

'It doesn't say much; the company's name is just mentioned among a number of prospective investors in next-generation energy projects that are being considered by the Nordic states,' she explained, tilting her phone so that Xander and I could see the photo she'd taken.

She was right – the article itself was little more than a paragraph and the words 'GreenSword Investments' were buried in the middle of it, with a bunch of other company names. How she spotted it turning the pages at the rate she does, I had no idea.

Xander jabbed his straw into the bottom of his glass, sucked up the last of his smoothie and sat back. 'It's something to go on, at least,' he said. 'I'll look into all the companies mentioned and see if I can find out what these "next-generation projects" are all about.'

'The more detail the better,' I said. 'I want to know as much as I can before I meet the guy. That way, I'll be able to tell if he lies to me.'

'Back up a bit,' said Xander. 'You're meeting him?'

I looked out of the window at the willow; it's always the first tree in the garden to sprout leaves, but the buds hadn't developed yet. The tree's thin bare branches were lashing about in the wind. It was a harsh day. Trying to sound as nonchalant as I could, I said, 'Yeah, I thought I would.'

Amelia narrowed her eyes. 'That doesn't compute.'

'Why not?'

'I thought the idea was to see what he gets up to when he doesn't know he's being watched. If you let on that we're cyberstalking him, he'll get more secretive still.'

'I'm not about to let on though, am I?'

'If you turn up asking questions, don't you think he'll guess?'

I hadn't told Amelia or Xander my deeper reason for wanting to know more about Armfield. Like them, I was keen to find out what he'd really been up to among the child soldiers of Somalia. We all felt for Mo and the other kids we'd been held alongside in the training camp. Armfield had helped us get out – for a fee, we assumed, though Mum later disputed that. Either way, because of him, many more kids had gone to the frontline. We'd seen him buying them for the war with our very own eyes. On the face of it, the guy was pure evil: he needed exposing.

Amelia and Xander knew he'd delivered us to Mum. But they didn't know what she'd tried to tell me: that the man was in fact my biological father. They didn't know he'd written to me asking to meet, either. And I wasn't about to tell them. Not unless he turned out to be for real. I'd tell them everything then.

For now, I just said, 'Look, I may not have your speed-reading skills, Amelia, or your ability to navigate the dark web, Xander, but I have a brain. Armfield got in touch with Mum when we were being held hostage. She's no idiot either. She'll have kept a record. I know the password for her laptop and I can check her contacts file. I'm pretty sure I'll find a number for him.'

In the pause that followed this little speech, Amelia and Xander looked at one another. Before either of them could say anything, a hollow *whump* sounded outside the kitchen window. It was just the empty wheelie bin being blown over by the wind, but it made me jump. I was wound pretty tight. And I knew why. It wasn't just that I was going behind Mum's back with my plan; I'd only been half truthful to Amelia and Xander as well, and that didn't feel right either. It was what it was though. I got up from the island and headed for the back door, saying, 'Better sort that before the wind blows it out into the road.'

# 7.

I didn't actually have to snoop around Mum's laptop for Armfield's contact details; they were on the note he'd sent me when we returned from East Africa. I'd kept it, of course. That evening I texted him: *if the offer still stands, I'd actually be on for meeting*. He wouldn't necessarily recognise my mobile number so I added *jack courtney*.

*Sure: London, Thursday?* came his instant reply.

*narrow it down a bit* I texted back.

*Steps in front of National Gallery, 14.00.*

*i'll be there*

It takes less than an hour to get into Central London from where Mum and I live in the Surrey hills, but the train I boarded was one of those rattly local ones that stopped frequently and seemed to have a problem getting back up to speed every time it pulled out of a station. It was another bleak day: purple-brown clouds dumped heavy rain on the grey fields as we inched along. The wind, thrashing the rain against the train windows, made it feel rattlier still.

I reread the message Xander had sent me that morning. He'd uncovered some more detail about the Nordic next-generation power project thing. I'd been through it all carefully already; I wanted to have the details at my fingertips before my meeting with Armfield. At the rate my train was going, I started to worry that I'd miss him. But I'd built in some extra time for the journey, and not just in case I got delayed; I wanted a chance to get to the National Gallery ahead of Armfield to find a spot where I could wait and watch for his arrival.

I jogged from Waterloo station to the broad stone steps in front of the gallery to make sure I was there first, but he'd beaten me to it. As I was looking for somewhere dry and out of the way to put myself, he tapped me on the shoulder. 'Hi there, Jack.'

I spun around, hot from the jog, wet from the rain, and annoyed to have been jumped like that.

'It's good to see you again,' he said, reaching out and patting me on the shoulder. 'Shall we go inside?' he asked, nodding at the gallery entrance, 'and get out of the rain?'

I can't explain why, but every bone in my body ached with the urge not to go along with him. I didn't like that he'd touched me, and I wanted to insist we stayed outside, rain or no rain. Something about the guy just didn't seem right, but I felt compelled to do as he asked. An irresistible force pulled me after him as he turned and headed swiftly up the slick steps.

In Somalia he'd worn khaki and looked like a soldier. Today he was in jeans, trainers and a waxed jacket with the collar turned up. He seemed younger and more athletic. I hurried to keep up with him as he strode between the huge stone pillars of the massive entrance porch. We could have stopped there to talk – the checked tile floor was sheltered from the rain – but he walked into the museum. He didn't stop when he got inside either. You don't have to pay to go into the National Gallery. With a nod to the attendant, he strode on, trailing me in his wake. He didn't slow down until we reached a huge picture of a horse rearing up on its hind legs. There was a long leather bench in the middle of the room. Armfield sat on it and motioned for me to join him. I did so, at a distance.

'I'm pleased you decided to meet me,' he said.

His eyes were grey and clear; it felt like he could see inside me. I had to look away.

'What has your mother told you about me?' he asked, his voice low. 'Let's start there, shall we?'

I stared at the rearing horse. The veins were visible in its raised forelegs; its haunches pulsed with power; there was an untameable madness in its glinting eye. I wasn't about to let this man dictate everything. Instead of answering his question, I turned to face him again and asked one of my own. 'What are you doing for GreenSword Investments?'

He blinked once.

I followed up immediately with, 'And while we're at it, what were you really doing in Somalia?'

'I hoped I'd explained that in my letter,' he said.

He'd ignored my first question and didn't elaborate on his answer to the second.

'You gave an explanation of sorts,' I said. 'It was pretty vague.'

'It was the truth. I was working to shut down child-soldiering camps like the one you got yourself caught up in, run by General Sir.'

'By buying kids from him and sending them off to war?'

He sighed and ran his fingers through his short brown hair. 'Come on, Jack, what are we really here to talk about?'

'That,' I said simply, and looked back at the horse. It was so lifelike, yet the painter hadn't included any background. There was no rider, no saddle, no bridle; the horse was alone, rearing up in infinite space.

'What can I do to prove it to you?' he said gently.

'You can give me more detail. Who were you working for, for example?'

'Why does that matter?'

'Because it does. In the same way that I want to know what you're doing for GreenSword Investments now. I want to know who you are and what you do.'

'I thought we were here . . .' he began, then tailed off, shook his head and looked from me to the painting. A Japanese couple had stopped to look at it too. They were wearing identical trousers – the sort that zip off at the knee to become shorts. They were also wearing headphones, no doubt listening to a recorded tour that explained who had painted the horse, when and why. I wouldn't have minded knowing myself. Was Armfield pausing because he didn't want to be overheard? The headphones made the chance of that pretty unlikely. I sat there listening to the hush, taking in the floor-polish smell, waiting.

Eventually he said, 'OK. I'm an intelligence and security contractor. Way back in history I trained with and worked for the British government, but now I work for myself. Which means I have many varied clients. In Somalia I was helping a Swiss charity. GreenSword is an entirely different job. I'm impressed that you found out about my involvement with them, by the way. It's pretty recent. They're an interesting new outfit looking to invest in energy projects. The stakes are high in that world. There are some tricky situations to negotiate. As there were in Somalia, I think you'll agree. That's the only link between the two jobs. I take on challenging projects I believe in: that's about it.'

His face was open and friendly and his voice was low and warm as he gave this explanation. Why then couldn't I trust him? The stuff he'd said about the Swiss charity was the only news to me. He'd told me less about GreenSword than I already knew. He'd not specified where these energy projects were or mentioned sustainability, for example.

I looked back at the painting. Although it was utterly realistic the painter had in fact blurred the horse's outline in places, ever so slightly. It was rock solid, utterly still, and somehow, at the same time, moving.

'What's the Nordic next-generation power project about?' I asked.

He puffed out his cheeks. 'Wow, you really have done your research,' he said. 'To be honest, I don't have a lot of detail yet. The client is in the early stages of investigating opportunities in that region.'

That hardly seemed likely. From messages Xander had hacked, I knew that Armfield was booked on a flight to Helsinki the following week. He wouldn't be setting off without knowing what he was going to do, would he? I looked back at the painting, at the panicked eye and flared nostrils of the rearing horse, the electricity in its muscles. The thing radiated strength.

'It's good, isn't it?' Armfield said.

I glanced at him and saw he was indeed looking at the painting. He went on. 'Apparently George Stubbs – the painter – showed the picture to the horse, who was called Whistlejacket, and when Whistlejacket saw it he reared up to fight. He must have seen the picture of himself as a rival stallion or something.'

'Huh.'

'Legend has it that the painting was intended to end up as a portrait of King George III. He was supposed to be sitting on top of Whistlejacket or holding his reins, and the pair of them were to be set against a rural landscape. But when the horse reacted as it did to the painting, the rich guy who commissioned it was so impressed that he told Stubbs to put down his brushes and hang it up just as it was.'

'So, it's unfinished.'

'If the story is true, yes. Either way, I like the painting as it is.'

Despite myself, I nodded. Had he planned to bring me here to see this particular artwork? Was Whistlejacket supposed to represent something? I had no idea, but bonding over the painting with Armfield was making me feel uncomfortable.

I changed the subject, saying, 'You must know more about GreenSword than that.'

'I know they intend to invest in new sustainable power projects in the Nordic region,' he said.

'Sustainable?'

'Wind farms, hydroelectric, solar, nuclear.'

'And your contract is to help them do that how exactly?'

He was doing a good job of looking bemused by my questions, but there was something slick about his answer. 'My role is twofold. I'm assisting with the due diligence – intelligence-gathering on potential investments and so forth – and I'm helping with security, ensuring the company's representatives are kept safe.'

'I didn't realise that countries like Norway and Finland were so dangerous.'

'They're not especially. But Finland borders Russia and there are oligarchs with interests in the region's power supply. Some of them can be . . . pretty unscrupulous. Really, though, this is just a routine contract for me.' He smiled. 'Trust me, it's nothing out of the ordinary. Why are you so interested, anyway?'

I wasn't about to answer that, not directly, but I still surprised myself with what I said instead. It came out of my mouth before I could stop it. 'I just am. You want me to trust you? Well, let me come to Helsinki with you. Show me what you do first-hand.'

His smile faded. His face became unreadable. I felt

strangely frightened, like I'd decided to play chicken with an unstoppable force. Again, he seemed to be staring right into me, weighing me up. I hadn't expected to ask him that question. I knew there was no way he'd let me tag along, and with every passing second I was less sure I wanted to. I just needed him to see that he would have to earn my trust with something more than a few reassuring words in front of a picture of a horse. I certainly didn't expect him to answer the way he did.

'You want to come and see what I do? Well, you'll appreciate that I can't take you into every meeting I have. The client wouldn't put up with that. But if it matters that much to you, and if it means you'll take me seriously, I'll take you along and show you what I do as best I can.'

'Really?'

'If your mother agrees, and if you can get the time off school.'

'There's two weeks of the Easter holiday left, and I reckon I can persuade her.'

He breathed in through his nostrils, held the breath for a second, and breathed out with a slow nod. 'Then . . . yes.'

# 8.

A stillness descended in the gallery after Armfield said yes. The Japanese couple had moved on and we had the room – and the monumental Whistlejacket painting – to ourselves for a moment.

'Right then,' I said, checking my phone. 'We'll have plenty of time to talk on the trip. I'd better get home now. Text me with the details.'

He nodded again and said, 'Yes sir,' amusement in his eyes.

I had nothing in particular to be getting home for, but since he'd surprised me at the start of the meeting, I wanted to be in charge of how it ended. I returned his nod as I stood up then walked away slowly, trying to appear calm. In fact, my pulse was flickering in my neck. It annoyed me that the guy put me so much on edge.

On the train home I thought about the meeting, trying to make sense of it. He'd agreed to take me with him on his business trip. Wasn't that proof enough that what he was doing was above board? Not quite: he'd said I could go with him, but he'd also told me there'd be stuff I couldn't be part of. We'd see about that.

He obviously wanted to get to know me. Well, that made sense if what Mum had nearly said (I'd cut her off – I didn't want to hear it) about him being my biological father was true. She had no reason to lie to me and he had no reason to reach out, but I still didn't have to accept the fact. I'd only do so when I was absolutely sure I wasn't about to be burned again.

I'd push him, see how far his openness and generosity went, make sure he was for real before I risked that. I couldn't quite put my finger on it, but something about his willingness to say yes to my request made me more suspicious of him, even as it felt like a good thing. Part of me was impressed; part smelled a rat.

I messaged Xander and Amelia: *Asked to go with him to finland and he said yes.*

Xander replied straight away. *Yeah, right. Assume we get to come too?!*

And Amelia immediately added, *If so, I'll need help with the funding.*

I smiled to myself. Xander was joking. Amelia wasn't. She's not the best at spotting a gag, even when it's obvious. But as I was thinking of a witty reply the train ran between high embankments and the roar of the engine immediately took me back to the moment before the second slab of avalanche hit me.

As they had before, Amelia and Xander had been my back-up then. Without them, I'd be dead.

I deleted the opening *ha ha ha* of my draft text and typed instead, *Sure, why not?*

Later that evening, the three of us met online. Amelia was in her bedroom sitting in front of a wall of unfluffy-looking books. I knew the sort of titles – *A Brief History of Tomorrow*, *Trends in Contemporary Trust Law*, *Virus Taxonomy*, *Europe at War* – piled on her shelves without having to read them. Xander was in the expansive kitchen of his parents' second home – not the one with marble columns in Nairobi, but their red-brick London townhouse in Pimlico. His dad is into abstract art; the wall Xander had chosen to sit in front of held a huge swirly painting the colour of tarmac and cement. Each to their own, I guess.

'Were you serious?' Amelia asked straightaway. Like I said, she's not the best at getting when people are joking. The flip side of that is that she doesn't care at all and always dives straight in and asks if she's unsure.

'Yeah,' I said.

'Good,' she said. 'I've been working on that assumption.'

Xander laughed softly. 'But he'll never agree to it. Why would he?'

'It's not like he doesn't know who you are,' I said. 'He helped us all escape in Somalia.'

'So what?' said Xander. 'That means we owe him, if anything. The debt definitely doesn't flow the other way.'

'He's right,' Amelia acknowledged. 'But still, what we need is a parallel purpose out there. It doesn't have to be real, just convincing. I've been giving it some thought.'

I leaned forward. 'What have you come up with?'

'We know he's flying into Helsinki. The bit of the message chain that Xander managed to uncover suggests they'll be heading up north. There was mention of a boat – a ship, really – called the *Polar Flow*. I've looked it up. It seems to be a research vessel of some sort, an ice-breaker. What they're chartering it for, I don't know, but I thought we could say we want to make a film of the journey to go with the stuff we shot in the Alps. You know, developing the global warming angle. On the Brink, et cetera.'

'Maybe see if we can get out into the tundra and shoot a snowscape that isn't trying to wipe me out,' I said, as much to myself as them. Amelia's plan seemed a good one to me. Mum would be likely to back us contributing to her cause. If Armfield agreed to let us film with him, that is.

'It's better than nothing,' said Xander. 'But it needs some work. If we knew precisely where he was headed, I could try to come up with something more specific.'

'Let's all give it some thought,' I said. Mum's car had crunched to a stop on the drive; in seconds she would be coming through the kitchen door. 'Gotta go now. Talk soon.' I shut my laptop screen.

Mum brought a blast of cold air into the kitchen along with our cat, Geoff, whose fur was beaded with rain. He mewed loudly at us.

'Did you not hear him asking to come in?' she asked.

I had not. Geoff normally comes and goes through the window we leave ajar in the utility room, but when the weather is savage Mum sometimes closes it – normally after checking that Geoff is in. Whose fault was it if Geoff had

had to put up with a spell outside? Mum had also been rain-lashed in the short dash from her car to the kitchen. She dropped her bags on the mat, unpeeled her coat and hung it, dripping, on a peg on the door, saying, 'Good day?' with a hopeful smile.

I decided to cut her some slack. She's tirelessly optimistic, totally committed to her environmental campaigning and yet also generally worried – for me, the country, the planet – at the same time. It struck me that she would be pleased to hear about the unexpected development between me and Armfield. What's more, she might be able to influence him over the whole Xander-and-Amelia thing.

'Yeah, as a matter of fact, today's been all right. I met up with Jonny Armfield' – it seemed right to use his 'real' name with her – 'and it went pretty well.'

Slowly, she turned towards me and surveyed me, taking stock with a little nod. I could tell she didn't want to look too enthusiastic too soon; I don't understand why, but when she does that it generally pushes me the other way and she knows it.

'Where? When? What did you . . . discuss?' she asked.

'Some gallery in London, this lunchtime, and just . . . stuff,' I said.

'I see.' She was obviously dying to ask for more detail, but knew better than to press me. 'Cup of tea?' she asked instead.

I felt selfish. Whatever she'd been out doing in the rain, it wouldn't have been for herself. For Mum, other people always come first.

'Sit down,' I said, pulling out a chair. 'I'll make it.' As I boiled the kettle and dug out our least-chipped mugs I said casually, 'Yeah, he was decent to me. Even offered to take me with him on his next overseas trip. You know, for work experience, and an opportunity to get to know one another. He has a client in Finland, I think . . . or Norway.'

'When?' she asked cautiously.

I waited until I was handing her the tea before looking at her. Sure enough, there was concern in her eyes. I hadn't been expecting that.

'Soon. Leaving sometime next week, in fact.' Trying to sound upbeat, I went on, 'It's in the holidays, at least. And the project he's working on is to do with sustainable energy. With any luck I'll be able to get some footage for our On the Brink film.'

Mum sipped her tea then slowly placed the mug on the kitchen table. 'I see,' she said, pressing her fingertips together. 'And he offered to take you, did he?'

I don't know why, but it was easier for me to nod than tell her that I'd asked to go.

'Kind of him,' she murmured, looking out of the window. I'd thought she would be happy, but her brow was furrowed with concern. 'I'm sure he'll keep you safe, but make no mistake, his world is pretty full-on. You'll need to keep your wits about you.'

'The film idea, though. You're happy about that, surely?'

'Oh, yes.' She said this quietly and, perhaps surprised by the lack of conviction in her own voice, repeated more emphatically, 'Oh yes.'

## 9.

That evening I took my time writing another message to Armfield. Whichever way I phrased the request – for him to allow Amelia and Xander to come on the trip – seemed destined to fail. Reading my penultimate attempt back to myself, I realised that my politeness – all proper punctuation, capital letters, and even an 'I await your considered response' sign-off – made me sound like a stiff, desperate idiot.

So I deleted it. I typed *Long shot, but can I bring three friends? we're making a film – i can explain* – then pressed send straight away. Sometimes it's best to shoot from the hip. At least that was honest and sounded like me.

'Three' wasn't a typo. As well as Amelia and Xander, I wanted my cousin, Caleb, on this trip. I hadn't seen him since our disastrous time in the Democratic Republic of Congo. He'd been his usual cocky self when we left for that trip, and to start with I'd have done pretty much anything to get shot of him. But he'd changed. When push came to shove, he'd put himself on the line for us, even standing up to his bully of a father – my Uncle Langdon – on our behalf.

Without Caleb's help we'd never have been able to escape from Langdon's tantalum mine, Canonhead. Caleb had fought his father hand to hand to help us get away, and taken a physical beating for his trouble; what punishment Langdon had inflicted on him since I didn't like to imagine. I'd been looking for a way of making it up to my cousin. It had occurred to me that this might be it.

Within minutes my phone vibrated with an incoming call. It was Armfield. I let the phone pulse three times before answering. Given the speed at which he'd answered, I half-expected the sort of exasperated 'Don't push your luck' 'Dad' would no doubt have dished out. But instead, without wasting time on pleasantries, Armfield said, 'Explain the film project to me.'

I did, making Mum's involvement in the On the Brink project clear. Although I didn't know – or want to know – how close they were, I was sure they'd been in touch since we got back from East Africa. He probably knew all about the initiatives she was working on anyway.

I'd got up from the sofa when I answered the phone, and I was pacing up and down the hall. There's a red rug with a pattern on it in the middle of the black-wood floorboards in the hall. I stared at it as I paced, my voice low and – hopefully – persuasive. The rug is old and pretty threadbare, and I'd never before realised that the repeating stylised pattern on it was of archers taking aim at a stag.

When I finished, he said, 'There's a bit of fieldwork on this trip, but you realise much of it is just meetings in cities, negotiations in offices, which you guys can't attend?'

I liked that he'd said 'you guys'; it made me feel hopeful.

'Of course,' I said, and played the only card I had. 'But if you're taking the *Polar Flow* up towards the ice pack, or even into it, I'm sure we could get some amazing footage then.'

'The *Polar Flow*.' He didn't sound angry that I knew about the ship, more bemused. 'How on earth do you know about her?'

'Between the three of us, we're pretty good at working things out,' I said.

'So it seems.'

'We'll still have a proper opportunity to talk,' I said, meaning him and me. 'And Xander, Amelia, Caleb and I might get something worthwhile done when you're tied up with the other stuff.' I upped the ante with a twisted half-truth. 'Mum's pretty keen on us contributing to the whole On the Brink project.'

'You're asking a lot here, Jack,' he said.

'I know,' I replied, and left it at that.

There was a pause. Maybe what I was asking was impossible, or more likely he just didn't want to do it. I stared at my bare feet. They looked pale against the rich red rug spread out beneath them. None of the archers had hit the stag yet, I noticed. In each repeating pattern sequence the tiny fleck of an arrow was suspended, mid-air, sailing towards its frozen target. I cast about for something persuasive to add, but could come up with nothing. Hope fizzled out and a hollowness spread through my chest. I was surprised when he eventually said, 'Let me get back to you. I'll see what I can do.'

It sounded like he meant it.

# 10.

I heard nothing for two days. My optimism faded. I hardly knew Armfield and certainly didn't trust him, but I'd seen enough of him in Somalia to know that he wasn't the sort to mess about. He'd said he would see what he could do; it seemed he'd had time to think and had decided that the answer was 'nothing'. I'd probably ruined my own chance of going with him on this trip by pushing him to include the others. What an idiot.

I hate waiting for things to happen. I'm rubbish at it: impatience is one of my worst traits. But I knew there was no point hassling the guy. Rather than just sit at home staring at my phone, I took our dog, Chester, out biking to distract myself. He knows the trails as well as I do, so I wasn't that worried when I pulled up at the bottom of Barry Knows Best, a trail he's followed me down a thousand times, to find that he wasn't with me. He's eight now, not as quick – or as nuts – as he used to be, and I'd hit Barry Knows Best pretty hard.

While I was waiting for Chester to catch up, I cleaned the mud from my goggles and stretched my back. Above me the bare branches were still against the white sky. I called Chester's name and was just about to take my gloves off, stick my fingers in my mouth and give him a proper get-here-now whistle when my phone went off in my backpack.

Armfield launched right in as soon as I pressed answer.

'Right then,' he began. 'I have a proposal for you. You want two things. First, for me to prove I'm on the side of the good guys. Second, a chance for you and your friends to film in the wilderness for your mum's On the Brink project. I've consulted GreenSword. Unsurprisingly, they're not prepared to let you attend sensitive negotiations. But they are happy for me to introduce you to their team on the trip and they'll answer your questions. So, prepare some good ones.'

'I will,' I said.

'What's more, they want to help fund your film. I'm not that surprised. Supporting a worthy cause makes them look good. Creative kids combatting climate change: it's a winner for them. You just have to give them a credit.'

'That's amazing,' I said.

'It gets better. We've put together an itinerary for you. Up north. It involves dog-sledding, ice fishing, snowshoeing, cross-country skiing and snowmobiling. You'll even get to build an igloo and sleep in it. Sound good?'

I swear Chester reappeared as Armfield said 'dog-sledding'. He padded over and rubbed himself against my knee. This was incredible news. There had to be a catch. I slipped my fingers into the warmth of Chester's neck fur, waiting for it to come.

'Speechless, eh?' Armfield said. 'Well, you should be. But it won't be a complete picnic, trust me. You'll be put through your paces.'

Was there a hint of a threat in this, or a challenge at least? Either way, I'd meet it.

'I'll email you the details – timings, kit list, et cetera. Get yourselves equipped and be ready to board a six a.m. flight on Monday from Heathrow. OK?'

'OK,' I managed to say. 'Thank you.'

With that, the phone went dead. The woods felt eerily quiet. There was just the sound of Chester panting beside me. He'd evidently exerted himself. Maybe he'd scented a deer and run off in search of it. Either way, he'd come back eventually, and was now looking up at me expectantly.

'What do you make of that?' I asked him. I didn't quite know myself. On the one hand I couldn't help feeling excited, but something was dampening my mood. Perhaps Xander or Amelia would be able to put a finger on it. I clipped on Chester's lead – he's pretty good at running next to the bike untethered, but if there were deer about I didn't quite trust him – shouldered my backpack and cruised home.

I didn't clean my bike or shower before getting hold of Xander and Amelia online. She immediately pointed that out. 'You claimed you'd be revising today, but the mud on your chin suggests you've done no such thing.'

It was true that we all had end-of-year exams coming up, and I had mentioned something about using the downtime to prepare for them, but as usual I had more important things on my mind. Amelia never revises: if she's looked at something once, she doesn't have to look at it again to remember it. I ignored her and ran them through what Armfield had told me.

'That's incredible news,' said Xander.

'It's almost as if he has something to prove,' added Amelia.

'Yeah,' I said. She was right, of course: although Armfield's offer was incredibly generous, it somehow felt like a gauntlet thrown down for me.

# 11.

Now that I had a real offer to put to him, I called Caleb. It turned out that his father, Langdon, had disowned Caleb for standing up to him at Canonhead. I wasn't surprised. My uncle is as crooked and unfeeling as his brother, the man I used to call Dad.

'When you say "disowned", what do you mean exactly?' I asked him over the phone

'He left me at Canonhead when he returned to Kinshasa, as you know. Literally had me sent down a mine. I had to bribe my way out.'

Either the line was bad or Caleb's voice had lost its force since I saw him last. He went on slowly. 'When I finally got back to the capital, he wouldn't let me through the front door. If it hadn't been for my mother, I'd probably still be stuck on the street out there. She sided with him, of course. But she got me back to London to finish school.'

I'd assumed he was still overseas. He certainly sounded far away. It came as a shock to learn that he was just up the road. I kicked myself for not having made contact earlier. If it hadn't been for me, he'd never have crossed his father in the first place.

'Look, Caleb, I'm sorry –' I began.

He interrupted me: 'No, no. After what our family put you through, it's me who should apologise. I'd have made contact myself, but from the radio silence I thought you probably didn't want to have anything more to do with any of us. Who could blame you? I'm just pleased if I was wrong. It's good of you to call.'

He sounded so unlike himself. I knew our time in the Democratic Republic of Congo had softened his arrogant edges, but what had happened since seemed to have hollowed him out entirely.

'If you're back in London it must be your Easter holidays,' I said.

With a sigh, he confirmed that it was.

'So, what are you doing?'

'Staring out of the window talking to you.'

'No, in general. Over the next couple of weeks.'

'I'll be stacking supermarket shelves half the time and staring out of the window some more for the rest of it, I guess.'

'Guess again,' I said, and filled him in on our trip to Finland. I explained about the film, but left out my deeper motive for going. Apart from a polite 'hmm' and an 'uh huh', he said nothing. I had to add a 'So, what do you think?' to get a response out of him.

'Sounds great. I'm sure you'll have a good time.'

'No – I mean, do you want to come?'

'Me?' he asked, incredulous.

'Yeah.'

It sounded like he had a lump in his throat when he replied. 'I'd love to, Jack. But –'

'No buts,' I said.

'There is one though. Money. Dad has obviously cut me off and Mum's not about to fork out for a holiday. I'm working part-time stacking shelves at Tesco but I've got no savings, no way to pay the airfare myself.'

'You won't have to,' I explained. 'GreenSword are footing the bill. It'll be good to see you, Caleb. I owe you.'

'You don't, but thanks.'

I ended the call and stood up from the kitchen table to see Mum in the doorway. How much she'd overheard I had no idea, but when I said I'd been speaking to Caleb she seemed pleased.

Later that day an email landed in my inbox with a description of what we'd be doing on the trip, and of all the stuff we'd need to take. I wasn't surprised by the military thoroughness of Armfield's preparation, but I hadn't expected his postscript, which read: *Remember – keep receipts for any kit the four of you buy: GreenSword to reimburse*. It seemed they were taking the whole backing-a-kids'-expedition-film thing seriously. I forwarded the email to Amelia, Xander and Caleb, and over the course of the next half hour they all replied.

Xander was first, with a gleeful *Get in there!*

Caleb's response came next: *Thanks for including me, guys. I won't let you down.*

And Amelia followed up with: *You've already demonstrated that, Caleb. As for GreenSword picking up the kit cost too: suspiciously generous?*

I knew what she was getting at: there's no such thing as a free lunch. But this was an international investment fund we were talking about. A few hundred pounds on warm clothes was nothing to them, and the publicity our film could generate was obviously valuable. I messaged back saying that.

Since time was tight, getting hold of the kit meant visiting an outdoor pursuits shop – the sort that sells climbing ropes and crampons, skis and ski boots, tents and stoves and GPSs – that day. I didn't need any of that, but I did come away with a new rucksack containing, among other things, a pair of snow boots, some thermal leggings, a rechargeable head torch and a four-season sleeping bag.

Sunday blurred past. I checked my cameras and made sure Xander did the same with his equipment, including the drone.

'Relax,' he replied.

Before I knew it, I was saying goodbye to Mum outside Heathrow's Terminal 2. She'd been pretty quiet over the last couple of days and looked a bit low now, about to wave me off.

'You're behind me on this, aren't you?' I asked.

'Definitely. I am,' she said.

Her brittle nodding undermined her words. I raised an eyebrow. 'Are you sure?'

She tried again. 'I'm pleased, yes, that you want to do your bit for On the Brink, and that you're reaching out to Jonny like this.'

'Good,' I said, giving her a hug.

She gripped my elbows, held on to me for a second, and said, 'Just –'

'I know. Be careful. I promise I will,' I said.

With that I headed across the concourse. Prolonged goodbyes are not a good thing. I knew Mum would perk up once she'd got into the swing of her day. She's a doer, like me, happier when she's busy, making a difference.

Amelia was already at the departure gate, as was Caleb. I did a double take when I saw him. He used to be much bigger than me, bulky with gym-built muscle. And the last time I'd seen him he had a crewcut. Now his hair was shaggy and he'd lost weight from his face, chest, shoulders – everywhere. He looked gaunt.

Had he been ill? Or was this simply what eight months of worry had done to him? I thought back to the kid so cocky he'd encouraged a gorilla to charge at us, with disastrous consequences. And I remembered him strong enough to fight his father, Langdon, a big, burly man. Caleb was wiry at best now, and there was a wariness about him.

I tried to put him at ease with a smile and a fist-bump.

'Technically we're supposed to check in a full two hours ahead of the flight,' Amelia said, looking at her phone. 'Meaning everyone else is late.'

This was true, and quite like Xander. He takes being laid back seriously. He strolled up with an hour to go today,

54

looking relaxed and, though it was five in the morning, well slept. His black hair was still wet from the shower, I noticed. From his house to the airport was little more than a fifteen-minute trip on the Heathrow Express.

He dumped his bag at our feet and nodded at Caleb as if he'd last seen him a day ago.

Minutes later, Armfield showed up in the distance. He strode towards us with the air of a man arriving at exactly the right time. I didn't realise until the last minute that the bearded man walking beside him wasn't just in step with him accidentally. Armfield had come accompanied. He nodded from his companion to me. 'Jack Courtney, meet Finn Macmillan, founding partner of GreenSword Investments.'

## 12.

I watched Finn Macmillan as we made our way onto the plane and took our seats. He had blond surfer hair and a beard. When I thought of city types, bloated grey men came to mind. Finn Macmillan was as skinny as Caleb and dressed in a checked shirt, faded jeans and Puma trainers. He didn't look much older than Sylvan, our ski guide in the Alps – early thirties at most. The only hint that he had money was his watch, a Rolex diver's model, that flashed from under his cuff as he fastened his seatbelt next to me. When he linked his hands and rested them in his lap it was still visible, the measured sweep of its second hand – no jerky ticking – as calm as he seemed to be.

I'm a pretty good judge of character; Finn Macmillan set me on edge instantly.

'So, Jack,' he drawled after the safety briefing had finished, 'Jonny's told me all about the film idea. Very cool. You're the director, right?'

We hadn't really assigned ourselves roles. If anything,

Xander came up with ideas for what we actually filmed. But I said, 'I suppose so,' anyway.

'Very cool,' he repeated, looking out of the porthole window. 'We're super-happy to help.'

This was my cue to acknowledge GreenSword's investment in us. I managed to say, 'Yeah, and we're very grateful,' but for some reason it didn't sound that sincere.

Macmillan had the window seat. I was next to him, and Amelia was fiddling with her phone on my other side. Caleb was across the aisle, with Xander and Armfield beyond him. A bit of help from Xander – who finds it easy to talk to just about anyone, and make that person feel good about themselves at the same time – would have been handy just then. I was tongue-tied. Macmillan was still turned away from me, apparently watching the runway rumble by, unconcerned. Without looking at me, he said, 'Jonny says you have some questions for us. Are they, like, for on camera, or are you thinking more of an informal chat?'

I hadn't considered an on-screen interview, but didn't want to admit that. 'Both, if possible,' I said, covering my bases.

'Sure,' he said, shifting in his seat. 'Go for it whenever.'

I hadn't expected to meet anyone from GreenSword so soon, and I'd been imagining a stiff, older, reluctant guy in a suit. Macmillan's casual American openness disconcerted me. I drew breath but before I could begin to speak the engines roared and the plane surged forward. As we shot down the runway, Macmillan took a pair of wireless headphones from his shirt pocket and slipped them into his ears. I didn't know whether he was listening to something or just using them to cancel out the engine noise. It seemed safest to wait until he took them out again before talking to him.

I glanced across the aisle as the plane climbed. Sure enough, Xander was chatting to Armfield like they were old friends. I couldn't hear what he was saying, but whatever it was it made Armfield laugh. Beside them, Caleb sat folded in on himself, staring at his fingers. Macmillan kept his headphones in until the breakfast trolley came around, when he took them out to order a cup of mint tea. He turned down the offer of a bacon roll, saying, 'Thanks, but no. The vegan option, please.'

It seemed a way in. As the trolley inched away, I asked him how long he'd been vegan.

'Six and a half years.' He smiled at me, nodding at the hot roll in my hand. 'And yeah, I do miss meat.'

'How long have you worked for GreenSword?'

'We set up formally last December,' he replied. 'But the idea has been kicking about for a few years.'

'What did you do before that?'

'This and that. Accountancy first, then an MBA at Harvard, some hedge fund work in New York. GreenSword is our opportunity to exert a positive influence.'

'Sustainable energy,' I said.

'For starters.'

'What exactly are you looking to invest in though? And why in the Nordic region?'

'Norway leads the world in hydroelectrics. And Finland has always been ahead of the curve on nuclear. They're looking to build more.'

'Nuclear power is classed as sustainable?'

'Yeah,' he said, sipping his tea. 'If it's done right, it is.'

I hadn't realised Amelia was listening, but she said, 'Fukushima and Chernobyl. Safe as . . .'

Macmillan nodded. 'They were catastrophic outliers. Nuclear is still our surest, cleanest route out of gas and oil until we've developed enough offshore – wind and tidal – alternatives. There's a plan to build the world's biggest wind farm way up in the Barents Sea. We're meeting some guys to discuss that this week too.'

'Is that why you've chartered the *Polar Flow*?' I asked.

'Partly,' he said. The plane hit a pocket of turbulence just then, but he didn't spill his tea. 'I'm looking forward to that bit of the trip,' he went on, sounding more like a tourist than a businessman. 'We'll get to see some ice, hopefully – the stuff we're fighting to preserve. I've not been to the Arctic before. You guys?'

I shook my head and Amelia said, 'No.'

'Well, it's going to be epic. I can't wait.' A smile played on his lips as he added, 'From what I gather, you guys are going to have your work cut out for you. Jonny's set you up a pretty challenging expedition.'

'We'll cope,' I said, and changed tack. 'What do you need Mr Armfield's help for, exactly?'

Macmillan shrugged. 'Deal-making around power, generated by any means, is a rough-and-tumble world. Noses get put out of joint. By all accounts, Jonny's a safe pair of hands.'

'So, can we film one of your meetings?' Amelia asked,

straightforward as a brick dropped into a pond. 'To get a sense of how these negotiations are done?'

Macmillan kept his gaze fixed on the wispy clouds we were whipping through. 'Sure,' he said. 'I thought you guys were going more for the nature angle, but I can try and get you a look at the boardroom nitty-gritty if you like, though I warn you it's pretty boring.'

With that he yawned, slotted the AirPods back into his ears, leaned back against the headrest. 'Whatever works best for you guys though, just say,' he said before shutting his eyes.

I exchanged a look with Amelia. Everything about this guy, from his Californian surfer look to his 'whatever' attitude, was unexpected. Unnervingly so: our conversation, and his positive response to Amelia's blunt request in particular, had felt too easy, like pushing against an open door.

Or was I just being stupidly suspicious? If Armfield was for real, and I took him at face value, why wouldn't Macmillan be relaxed and open with me? His company had agreed to fund our film. That was proof they supported what On the Brink was about.

Despite all that, I couldn't shift a nagging doubt: something wasn't quite stacking up.

# 13.

Things moved fast after we landed in Helsinki. We shot through passport control to find our bags somehow already on the baggage reclaim carousel. A white Mercedes people-carrier with blued-out windows rolled up as we exited the terminal building. Armfield raised a finger and it drifted to a stop beside us. Everything he did – even loading the bags through the big rear doors – was economical and deliberate.

Somehow, in the short time it had taken us to get from the plane to the car, Macmillan had already told Armfield he'd said we could sit in on one of his meetings. Once we were in the car Armfield, up front next to the driver, raised his phone to his ear and spoke into it with clipped precision. 'Lukas, Jonny, push the Rovaniemi connection to twenty-two hundred hours and cascade the itinerary accordingly.'

Amelia, seated between Xander and me, said, 'Rovaniemi is up north; it's the gateway to Lapland.'

Armfield, having ended the call, twisted around in his

seat and explained. 'Lukas is our in-country fixer for your trip. He's arranging transport and handling logistics. We've worked together before. It's always best to bypass tourist operators if possible: Lukas can be more responsive and adaptive. He's put together your overland trek.'

'Which starts from Rovaniemi?' asked Amelia.

'Thereabouts. We had planned for you to hit the ground running today, but Finn tells me you've convinced him to let you sit in on a meeting. Our twelve o'clock will give you a flavour of what a negotiation looks like.'

I checked my phone. Twelve o'clock wasn't far away.

'I'm afraid we can't have all four of you in the room,' Armfield went on. 'The consortium have agreed to two max. Which of you will it be? I'll text names ahead so they can prepare non-disclosure agreements for you.'

It went without saying that I'd be one of the two, but who should I take in with me? Amelia was the obvious choice. She'd have the best chance of filleting the facts out of whatever we heard. But Xander can read a room better than anyone I know – he'd identify who had the upper hand and see through people bluffing. Also, he's best with a camera.

'Can we film in the meeting?' I asked.

'Yes, but they'll want the right to approve anything you plan to include in the final cut.'

I figured they'd demand that, but it didn't matter. We could show Amelia whatever we shot, and let her pull out any important information we'd missed. I told Armfield to put my name and Xander's on the non-disclosure agreements. Finn Macmillan looked up from his iPad, nodded and said, 'Excellent choice' absently, as if approving of what I'd ordered for dinner.

'Caleb and Amelia, you can stay in the vehicle or do a bit of sightseeing,' said Armfield. 'Up to you. Just tell Karla here and she'll sort you out.'

The driver, Karla, a pale woman with short, white-blonde hair, had been threading the people-carrier into the grand heart of Helsinki. Big gothic edifices loomed around us. Xander, head down beside me, was inspecting his digital SLR/movie camera. He screwed it onto a pocket-sized tripod.

Amelia said, 'Who's this consortium, then?'

'It's made up of various industry players,' Macmillan murmured.

Amelia rolled her eyes. 'I don't suppose it has a name, does it?'

Macmillan turned in his seat, smiled and said, 'Valkoinen Karhu Energia.'

'Come again?' said Xander.

'She asked.'

'Something Energy,' said Amelia.

'Valkoinen Karhu,' Macmillan repeated, seeming to be enjoying the words.

There was a pause. I could almost hear the cogs in Amelia's brain whirring. Eventually she said, 'Karhu make running shoes. Their logo is a bear on a mountain, if I remember right. So: Bear Mountain Energy?'

'Wow,' said Macmillan. 'Impressively close. In fact, it's White Bear Energy. That's the consortium's translated name.'

We came to a halt beside a solid-looking old building.

63

The top two-thirds of it was painted dark yellow, while at street level its walls were grey stone. A tram rattled past us as Xander and I stepped down from the Mercedes. Amelia, I saw, was already on her phone, no doubt digging up whatever she could find out about White Bear Energy. Caleb, meanwhile, was staring at his fingers. He looked so diminished.

'See you in a bit,' I said, patting him on the arm.

'Sure.' He sighed.

I wanted to include him somehow, but couldn't think how to do it. A bigger challenge lay in front of me, through the doors of an anonymous city building miles from home. I had to focus on that. 'Let's go, Xander,' I said.

# 14.

Armfield was already leading the way into reception. I looked around as I followed him. There was no plaque beside the door and no company logo behind the reception desk. Two women in dark suits stood impassively behind it. They had similar hair: dark blonde and drawn up in a bun. Armfield dipped his head as he approached and said something I didn't quite catch, though I'm pretty sure it ended with the word 'karhu'. He barely slowed down for the reply, just ushered Macmillan between a pair of brushed-steel security bollards and across the marble floor towards the lifts.

Macmillan, I noticed, was whistling to himself while we waited for the doors to open. He looked like he was out for a country stroll, not about to attend an important meeting. Armfield, still scanning left and right, hit the seven button once we'd all stepped inside, and the lift duly spat us out on the seventh floor, into another reception area, where we were greeted by a tall bald man in a grey suit and open-necked white shirt. He wore glasses without rims. He blinked at us as he looked us up and down. If Macmillan was unnervingly cool, this guy's 'welcome' was outright cold.

'Hey, Timo,' said Macmillan, offering him a thumbs-up instead of shaking hands. Timo didn't look comfortable returning the gesture. Macmillan introduced Armfield as his advisor. Then, nodding at Xander and me with a smile, he said, 'Great of you to accommodate our mini media team. Don't mind them, they're just along for the ride.'

I liked the 'our' and 'team', but was less keen on the 'mini' bit.

Timo was carrying a tablet. He offered it to Xander, but Armfield intervened. After taking a look at the screen he handed it to me, saying, 'Digital signatures for the non-disclosure agreement, please.'

I knew that I should read the document before I signed it, but the certainty in Armfield's voice seemed to make that unnecessary. Nevertheless, I paused. Immediately he said, 'Take your time, but the NDA is fine. It's just a promise not to share anything without first having it approved. The rest is plain-vanilla boilerplate stuff.' His tone was reassuring, kindly even, but his words still made me feel out of my depth and pedantic. I had no clue what 'plain-vanilla boilerplate' meant. Flustered, I scrawled my name in the relevant box with my fingertip and passed the tablet to Xander. Needless to say, he looked unbothered as he followed suit.

With that, Timo led the way along an uplit, carpeted corridor lined with pale wooden doors, each of which had a window in it. I glimpsed tables and chairs but no people, not until we paused outside the last door on the right. It was ajar. Through the gap I heard voices. Timo pushed on in, and we followed.

This room was bigger than those we'd passed, spacious enough to accommodate a sizeable meeting table ringed by about twenty chairs. Half of these were occupied. Everybody stood up as Timo presented Macmillan. He was clearly the star of the show. That made sense: he had the money and these guys, with their potential investment projects, wanted it.

Armfield steered Xander and me into a corner, where somebody had set a couple of tall stools. A few of the suits glanced our way but they'd obviously collectively decided to ignore us. If Macmillan wanted us there, they had to put up with us.

The smell of coffee rose from a long sideboard beside us. On top of it were cafetières, teapots, cups and saucers, glasses, bottled water, soft drinks, platters of fancy sandwiches, even bowls of boiled sweets. I was hungry, but noticed that, apart from a few full coffee cups on the table, nobody appeared to have touched any of these provisions. In a space at the end of the sideboard nearest us Xander quietly set up his little tripod, checked the viewfinder's wide-angled take on the room, and set the camera to record before people had even re-taken their seats.

Armfield was the last to sit down. He did so once he'd circled the room. Somewhere along the way he'd picked up a pad and pencil, and he handed these to me before slipping into his seat next to Macmillan.

The meeting began. Everyone introduced themselves

formally. I was grateful for the pad. It gave me something to do: I drew a map of the table on it and jotted down the names as best I could. Everyone spoke English, apart from one guy with salt-and-pepper hair who had an assistant to translate for him. This translator looked younger than some of the kids in my year at school; he was scrawny and wore a black polo-neck beneath his suit jacket.

While the formalities were going on Macmillan rocked back in his chair, a knee pushing against the table, his hands behind his shaggy head. From where I was sitting, I had a good view of him side-on. He looked like he was barely listening. But after everyone had justified their place at the table, one of the only two women in the room began a presentation, and Macmillan's demeanour changed. His features, in profile, sharpened subtly.

The woman looked a little nervous; her long fingers wouldn't stay still. First she gave an overview of the Finnish energy sector, illustrated with a presentation projected onto one of the room's walls. She used lots of maps. I'm a fan of maps: I love their detail. For some reason, I find it easy to remember information I've seen on a map. These ones were beautiful, grey and white and blue, mostly detailing northern Finland, the Norwegian and Russian coastlines up by the Barents Sea, the archipelago of Svalbard, the Arctic ice pack and so on. The woman talked about exciting opportunities, rattling off costs and potential profits.

It seemed to me that Macmillan knew it all anyway: at one point he interrupted to correct a figure she'd quoted for the projected output of a new nuclear facility. The woman's hands paused, steepled, as she looked at her laptop, then sprang apart as she conceded he was right. She pressed on. He watched her closely, nodding now and then but taking no notes of his own, listening like an examiner rather than someone being taught.

Timo moved the meeting on to discuss wind farms, and a man with a puffy, unhealthy-looking face talked about kilowatts for a while. More than once I found I'd turned to look at the sandwiches. Armfield had been right; the meeting was pretty boring. He himself barely contributed. He sat a little back from the table, listening and watching, and only leaned forward when the translator slid a pair of folders across the table with the pompous announcement that they 'constitute our investment opportunity bible, for your perusal'.

'Thanks, we'll check them over,' Armfield said.

Next up was a man who blinked a lot. The puffy man introduced him as 'our granular details guy'. What did that mean? He seemed to talk in equations. The biggest was three lines long and combined carbon dioxide emissions with government subsidies, the price of construction materials, time, taxation rates and kilowatts per hour. I couldn't make head or tail of it but that didn't matter: we could show Amelia the film later. In school, equations make me glaze over. I was ashamed to find myself yawning. We'd had an early start. My rumbling stomach did a better job of keeping me awake than blinking equations man.

Xander fiddled with the camera once or twice. I could tell that he was as bored as I was. All I could work out was that these guys wanted to impress Macmillan and that as they were pitching to him, he was both focused and sceptical. The minute Timo said, 'Well, I think that wraps things up for now. Do you have any questions?' Macmillan pushed himself back from the table with his knee and morphed from unimpressed examiner to relaxed surfer, nodding and grinning his thanks, fist-bumping those within reach and paying no attention to Timo's concluding words about 'blue-sky green-wave opportunities', or 'overcoming stumbling blocks and laying down stepping stones going forward'.

Armfield stood up from the table, gathered the folders, and positioned himself to chaperone Macmillan – and us – from the room. Macmillan paused to choose a sandwich as he went. Was that a sign – accepting hospitality to show approval? Either way, I desperately wanted to join him and take one for myself, but something held me back. I hadn't the right somehow.

Hungry, tired and none the wiser, I trailed after Xander, Timo and Macmillan. Armfield brought up the rear as we headed back down the corridor and into the waiting lift. Timo's glasses flashed at us as he nodded goodbye. None of us spoke as the lift descended. Macmillan chomped on his sandwich, a faraway look in his eye. In seconds we were back on the pavement. I was just about to thank Macmillan – and Armfield – for letting us attend the meeting, but the people-carrier arrived and Armfield ushered us into it. Climbing into the front passenger seat, Macmillan smiled at us. 'Fun times, eh? Hope you got what you needed, boys. Welcome to my world!'

# 15.

I must have looked how I felt: dazed. When Amelia dug her elbow into my side and whispered, 'How did it go?', the best I could come up with was a shrug. I didn't know. If I'd had to guess at what such a meeting might look and sound like, that's what I would have come up with, more or less. Was that a reason to be suspicious? If I was a conspiracy theorist, maybe, but I wasn't one. At least we had the footage. Together, later, the four of us could watch it and see whether what Xander and I had witnessed was genuine.

Armfield, meanwhile, didn't seem to want to dwell on the meeting. He preferred to look ahead. Within seconds he was on the phone to Lukas, the in-country fixer, confirming our updated travel arrangements. We were booked on the same flight as him and Macmillan, heading north to Rovaniemi.

'We're doubling back to visit a proposed nuclear facility on the north Baltic coast, and you're heading north to get some film footage,' he said.

'Of what?'

'The works. As I said, I asked Lukas to put together a trek combining snowshoeing, cross-country skiing, snowmobiling and husky-sledding. Along the way you'll learn to ice-fish and build a snow shelter.'

'An igloo?'

'Yes – to sleep in. But don't worry, you'll be in cabins the other nights you're away. They're dotted along the tundra trails. And you won't have to rely entirely on your fishing skills for food; Lukas has sourced local provisions.'

'Local provisions?'

'Reindeer heart, walrus tongue, that kind of thing.' Armfield laughed. 'I'm kidding. Given the forecast, you'll have a good chance of filming the Northern Lights.'

It was impossible not to be grateful, though I still felt that something was amiss. 'Wow, thank you,' I heard myself say, despite myself.

'It'll be hard work,' he replied, deadpan.

Beside him, Macmillan chuckled. Though I hated myself for it, his nonchalance triggered a wave of apprehension in me. My 'We'll cope' sounded hollow.

'Sure you will,' he said.

Armfield shrugged. 'It's all for a good cause, eh? I'll rendezvous with you at the end of the trek in Hammerfest.'

'Hammerfest?'

'The Norwegian port. The *Polar Flow* will dock there. All being well, we'll nose up into the ice pack so you can capture some footage of that. I'm hoping we'll be able to take a look at one of the new offshore windfarms. They're what GreenSword is all about, after all.'

Having sped through our itinerary, Armfield turned around in his seat. The conversation was over for now. I didn't have a further opportunity to talk to him as we shot through the airport and onto the little plane that would take us north. It only had about thirty seats. We were dotted among them rather than sitting together, so I used the hour or so to catch up on some sleep. When we disembarked at Rovaniemi airport, Armfield hustled us through arrivals, where Lukas was poised to whisk us away. I'd imagined that Armfield might accompany us into town, but he and Macmillan, having left us in 'our fixer's capable hands', got into a waiting Mercedes, which immediately pulled away.

Lukas was forty-ish and very short, no more than five foot two, but he was solidly built and his hand, when he shook mine, had an iron grip. He was wearing a hat with fur earflaps. Behind him, a sign on the airport wall pointed the way to Santa Land. It was April. But that wasn't why I was feeling so confused; the speed at which Armfield had left us had rattled me.

'The truck's in the car park,' Lukas was explaining. 'We've a four-hour journey ahead of us. I have food and drink on board. Anyone need anything else before we set off?'

We looked at one another and shook our heads.

'Good, then let's get going.'

Within minutes we were in Lukas's Mercedes 4×4 heading north.

'What are we doing first?' Xander asked affably.

'Dogs,' was Lukas's one-word answer. The silence that followed made it clear he wasn't about to elaborate. Who was this guy? Armfield had simply left us with him, and now he was taking us into the wilderness. The truck's lights tunnelled into the darkness, illuminating a black strip of road bordered by banks of snow. I sat back, confused by what I'd witnessed that day, wondering what lay ahead.

# 16.

Eventually we came to a halt beside a couple of log cabins in the middle of what felt like the definition of nowhere. It was well after midnight. Dogs barked in the darkness. Lukas opened the door to one of the cabins. An unlit log burner stood in the corner and two sets of bunks were pushed up against the walls. We dumped our bags in a heap on the floor.

'Tikaani – the dog handler – must already have turned in for the night,' Lukas said, nodding at the other cabin. 'She will meet you first thing. Get some rest.' He retreated, shutting the door on us.

'Friendly chap,' said Xander.

'Not particularly,' replied Amelia, before the penny dropped. Once it had she said, 'Oh, I see.'

The Mercedes started up again immediately: he wasn't staying here with us, evidently. We looked at one another as the rumbling of the truck – and with it the barking – subsided.

'We might as well do as he said,' Caleb suggested, spreading his sleeping bag on one of the lower bunks. I took the one above him. Xander climbed onto the other high bunk. I couldn't get to sleep immediately, and neither could he, it seemed: his face was illuminated by his laptop screen and he had his camera in his lap. He was frowning.

'Something wrong?' I said.

'Bit of a glitch,' he said evasively. 'I'm sure it'll be fine.'

'What sort of a glitch?'

'I transferred the film of the meeting to my laptop, but the file is very small. When I open it, I can only see a minute's worth of footage. The first minute I filmed. That's not right.'

'Has it got compressed?' I said, knowing that Xander would have the answer.

'No,' he said. 'No.' He was tapping away at his keyboard, his look of concentration turning to disbelief.

'You're not serious,' I said.

'A minute's footage,' Amelia repeated below me.

'The file's been truncated somehow,' Xander said under his breath.

'Or you pressed "stop" too early,' she suggested.

Xander shot her a look. 'Yeah, I definitely did that. And I definitely didn't check and recheck that the camera was on, focused and filming the whole time.'

'So we've lost the footage?' I said, incredulous.

'We can't have,' said Xander. 'It's impossible. But . . .' His voice dropped. 'But, yes.'

Caleb said, 'Do you think someone's cut everything but the first minute of the film you took?'

'Looks like it. But who? The camera's barely been out of my sight.'

76

My stomach churned. What did this mean? Either Xander had made a mistake or somebody had tampered with our only evidence – apart from my few notes – of the meeting.

'Why not just delete the whole file?' Amelia asked.

'Because doing it this way makes it look like an operator mistake, not deliberate?' I suggested.

'Did you back up the file? Or upload it to the cloud?'

'No,' Xander said quietly.

'And the camera doesn't do that automatically?' asked Amelia.

'No.'

'You'd have been better off filming it on my phone,' she couldn't help saying.

'Thanks, Amelia,' said Xander, but without heat.

'Is there no way of retrieving the deleted footage?'

'I don't know. I won't give up,' Xander muttered, but he was shaking his head.

I took stock. We were in the middle of nowhere. Armfield had headed off in a different direction. I wasn't about to jump to the conclusion that he had tampered with the camera, but I couldn't believe that Xander had cocked up so royally either. It would be days before I could confront Armfield. In the meantime, I had no idea what he and Macmillan were really doing in Finland, who they were meeting, or what their real business interests were.

Something had felt off about the trip from the outset; now that feeling was stronger.

I reassured Xander that the missing footage wasn't vital. We'd witnessed the meeting; it was just a boring introductory this-is-roughly-what-we-have-to-offer pitch. Nobody had revealed any sensitive material, apart perhaps from the contents of the folders that had been slid across the table to Armfield. We'd see him again eventually. For now, I'd have to be patient.

Trying to boost my spirits wasn't working. Neither was my attempt to make Xander feel better.

'I should have backed up the file straight away,' he muttered.

# 17.

When I eventually slept that night, I dreamed I was back under the sea looking for treasure off Zanzibar. I found lots: rings, coins, even a gold bar. But it all crumbled to nothing in my fingers. At one point a seal swam alongside me. It turned its head as it went and barked in my face, waking me up.

In fact, the barking was coming from outside, and it didn't sound like just one dog. A chorus of yelping and yowling made me sit up in the top bunk. I'd forgotten I was in it, but bumping my head on the pine ceiling reminded me. I got up and dressed in long johns, overtrousers, a base layer, jumper, down jacket and snow boots, and headed outside to see what was bugging the dogs.

It turned out that the cacophony was a greeting of sorts. Not for us, or the morning – although the sun was just above the white horizon – but for a woman I assumed was Tikaani. She was preparing breakfast for the dogs, who were in an enclosure surrounded by a chain-link fence.

I called out a hello as I approached. The woman had her

back to me and was tipping steaming mush into a row of about thirty metal bowls. She didn't hear me at first over the noise of the dogs, but turned around when I called out a second time.

She was young, in her early twenties at most, with a shock of blonde hair pulled back in a messy ponytail, and she wore a thick-knit jumper with a diamond pattern around the neck. She nodded as I approached, but did not smile. I introduced myself and asked if she needed any help.

'You can take some of these over, if you like,' she said, pointing to the bowls at her feet.

'The dogs sound like they'd appreciate it,' I replied.

'Obviously,' she said, as deadpan as Lukas had been. It seemed that all Armfield's associates were as terse as each other.

All the dogs were outside, straining to greet us now. I placed a bowl of the steaming sludge down in front of the nearest one and ran my hand through the super-thick fur on his neck and back as he tucked in. My own dog, Chester, seemed a very long way away.

Returning to fetch more bowls, I saw that Caleb had come out of the cabin and was standing a little way off, his hands in his pockets. Once upon a time he'd have barged right in, but today he waited for me to wave him over. Between the three of us, we soon had all the dogs fed.

As we gathered up the bowls – they'd all been emptied in under a minute – Tikaani told us each dog's name. Two stood out to me: a mostly black dog called Victor and a little one named Mikka. Despite his dark colouring, Victor had the palest eyes: he seemed to stare right through me. Mikka was two-thirds his size, at most, and scruffy. She held her ears at comical angles and spun in circles as we approached. Despite her appearance, Tikaani explained, Mikka was the best lead dog in the pack.

'Even in a whiteout she finds the trail. All the others respect her. Remarkable animal,' Tikaani said.

Caleb knelt down in the dirty snow beside the dog. She immediately stopped spinning, cocked her ears and pushed her nose against his bent knee. Whether the dog could smell his resignation or see it in his posture I don't know, but I swear she was trying to comfort him. Tikaani noted it as well. 'Kind too. She likes you.'

Caleb, running his hand gently over the dog's bristly chin, said nothing.

'So, the dogs are fed, now it's our turn,' said Tikaani. 'Bring your friends to my cabin when you're ready for your breakfast.'

Amelia and Xander were up and dressed. Amelia's snow gear was electric orange, so bright it hurt to look at her in the morning sunshine. Xander's big fur-fringed parka, by contrast, was a sober grey. I didn't bring up the missing footage, but he wouldn't meet my eye: clearly he was blaming himself for having lost it.

Our breakfast looked a bit like the dogs', from a distance, but happily it was different. Their sludge was a rough soup of warm water, kibble, hunks of fat and bits of fish; our porridge swam with granola, chocolate, nuts and raisins, and was topped off with a generous slurp of syrup.

'There must be a thousand calories in this bowl,' Amelia said by way of thanks.

'You'll need them,' Tikaani replied. 'You've a tough day ahead.'

She'd opened the door of the wood stove to add another log, and a rush of heat pulsed into her cabin. Like ours, the single room was small and spartan, but she had a quilt on her bed and the table at which we sat was covered with a checked cloth.

'What's the plan, then?' asked Xander.

'This morning I will teach you about sled dogs. This afternoon we will make the first journey with them.'

'Do we get to drive our own?' I asked.

'You don't "drive" dogs, you "mush" them,' Amelia said.

'Correct.' Tikaani nodded and said to me, 'Of course. Mr Lukas insisted on it. Four sleds, four dog teams, and a challenging route. He said you are experienced adventurers: scuba-diving, skiing, jungle-trekking, yes? This will be no ordinary tourist trip.'

That Armfield – through Lukas – had organised this for us, struck me as extraordinarily generous. I couldn't help being excited, if a little nervous. Outside, something had triggered the dogs into another gale of barking. The sound was thrilling and insistent. It ran right through me.

Like the dogs, I wanted to get on the trip.

# 18.

After breakfast, Tikaani stood up and clapped her hands. 'Right. It's time to go.'

We crunched after her to an outbuilding that housed her equipment.

'First I'll show you the sled, then we can attach the dogs,' she said, dragging a dog sled out of the building.

'As you see, the sled sits on runners. They're like skis. But instead of wax on the bottom, we fit plastic strips. Different grades of plastic for different types of snow. The runners are fixed to the sled bed by stanchions.' She tapped a strut with her foot. 'They run on up to the handle-bow, with which you steer. Lean it this way or that, and the stanchions flex the runners to follow the dogs right or left.' She looked around at us. 'Now, here at the front, this black semi-circle of rubber is like a bumper to protect the sled if it runs into an obstacle. It's called the bush-bow.' Next she pointed to the red triangular middle section, which was made from the same sort of material as my rucksack. 'This is the sled bag. It sits on the bed, and it's for carrying equipment and supplies.'

Moving to the rear, she went on. 'You stand here, on cushioned footboards either side of the drag mat. Tread on the drag mat and you'll slow the sled – and the dogs – down. If you need to stop faster, you tread on this: it's called the bar brake. And to keep the sled in one place while you're not on it, we use a snow hook.' She picked up a vicious-looking metal claw attached to one of the stanchions by a rope. 'Stab it into the snow and the sled should go nowhere.'

'It's a fair bit to take in,' said Xander.

Amelia shot him a no-it's-not look. I have to say I agreed with her: everything made sense to me so far.

'And this cloth box here,' Tikaani continued, 'at the very back of the sled, is called the tail dragger seat. In it, we keep food for the dogs. You can sit on this if you get tired, as long as the sled is under control.'

'How do we connect the dogs?' asked Caleb quietly.

'With the bridle and gang-lines,' Tikaani answered. 'The bridle is the long rope that runs under the sled bed, through this fixing here, and on towards the team. Shorter gang-lines are attached to it at intervals, one for each dog. So, for today, you'll each have six. Let's get some out, shall we?'

As we followed her back to the compound, Xander fell into step with me and Caleb.

'The only time the camera was out of my sight was on the flight north,' Xander said. 'It was in the overhead locker then.'

'I slept on the plane,' I replied. 'Did you?'

'I don't remember.'

'You did,' Caleb observed. 'And Armfield walked up and down the aisle more than once.'

'You saw him mess with my luggage?' Xander couldn't keep the accusation out of his voice. 'And you did nothing about it?'

The old Caleb would have shot something vicious back, but all he said now was, 'No. I mean, I have no idea. If I missed it, I'm sorry.'

'Nobody needs to apologise,' I said, giving Xander a look.

'Except me,' he conceded.

We'd arrived at the dogs. Tikaani chose four, handing us one each by the collar. Mine, a deep-chested brindle male called Novak, bucked in excitement and swivelled to lick my face as I led him to the sled.

Tikaani brought two dogs herself, one of them little Mikka. She showed us how to fit a harness (each dog had its own), slipping it over the dog's head and carefully drawing each foreleg through. As she'd explained, the harness connected the dog to the bridle via gang-lines, but the dogs were also kept in place by a slimmer, non-weight-bearing lead that ran from the bridle to their collar.

'Mikka here is up front with Ace,' Tikaani said. 'They are this team's lead dogs. The most experienced, the best at following commands. Next come Alta and Buzz in what's called the swing position. And at the rear, closest to the sled, sit Novak and Kona. This is the wheel position. They take the first strain of pulling, so they need to be strongest.'

'Lead, swing, wheel,' Amelia repeated.

'That's right.'

'And how do we control them?' Xander asked, sounding mildly interested.

'There are four main commands. "Hike" means go. "Haw" means turn left. "Gee" means turn right. And "whoa" means stop. I use "all right" when they respond properly, so that's a fifth, I suppose.'

'What about "mush"?' asked Xander.

Amelia, clearly unable to help herself, turned to explain. 'Mush originally came from the French word *marche*. It's considered a bit soft, now. Doesn't cut through the wind as well as "hike". Dog sled drivers are still called mushers though. Go figure.'

Tikaani looked interested. 'You've done some research,' she said.

Amelia shrugged. 'Not really.'

We moved on. Having prepared one sled, Tikaani now demonstrated how to use it, instructing us to jog alongside and observe her at first, and then take turns having a go ourselves. Even though it was cold, running in snow gear meant we soon worked up a sweat. Steam rose from us when we stopped. I felt like the panting dogs. They clearly wanted to keep going.

By mid-morning Tikaani's instruction was over. We knew what to do in theory and had put it into practice, if briefly. I have to admit I was a bit nervous of simply launching down the trail once we'd hooked up the other sleds. But that's what she intended. Over a lunch of hot chocolate, salami and cheese eaten in the warmth of her cabin, Tikaani showed us a map of our route. I studied it carefully, but could only see that we were to spear straight into what looked like remote wilderness.

'You're coming too, right?' Xander asked Tikaani, for once sounding a little uncertain.

'No, you go alone,' said Tikaani. She seemed so matter of fact I actually believed her. But she continued, 'Of course I'm coming. I'm the guide. We're heading for this cabin here.' She pointed at a dot on the map with the tip of the cheese knife.

'That's . . . what? About thirty kilometres away?' I asked.

'Thirty-three. The dogs can cover many more than that in a day. Our only issue is the weather. It was set to be clear, but I learned this morning that we may have more snow on the way.' She puffed out her cheeks and said, 'Still, no big deal. Meet me at the sleds with your kit and you can help re-harness the dogs. I want to be under way within thirty minutes. OK?'

# 19.

Wrapped up from woollen-hatted head to ski-sock-and-snow-booted toe, and with goggles to help against the glare and wind, we were heading out into the snowy wilderness well within Tikaani's thirty-minute deadline, each of us pulled by our own team of sled dogs.

The hiss of the snow under the runners; the muffled padding of the dog's feet, and their panting; the gentle clattering of buckles and clips; the faint musky smell of the dogs and the clear, cold wind in my face; the effort of balancing on the footboards and deploying the drag mat and leaning into the corners, steering the right course, holding the correct pace, keeping everything in check and balanced; hiking, hawing, geeing and whoa-ing the dogs at the right time – it was all engrossing.

Tikaani led the way. Our dogs were no doubt following her. But it seemed that they responded to the commands I called out after she had given hers. The trail was hard-packed at first. It ran between frosted trees and bushes laden with snow. The sky was white-blue, whisked with clouds. When we hit an incline, Tikaani ran behind her sled to ease the dogs' burden. I copied her. Running was punishing work dressed in all that heavy kit, but it felt fair: though the dogs seemed to have limitless energy, they had to be hurting. Compared to them I was barely doing anything, but within a few hours I was feeling the strain of hanging on and balancing and running in the snow in my back, arms and legs.

In a clearing, we paused. The dogs instantly began nipping at the fresh snow. It was theirs to drink. I checked the GoPro camera that I'd strapped over my hat. Tikaani saw me and said, 'You mentioned filming with a drone too?'

'Yeah,' said Xander.

'Well, now's your chance, before the weather closes in,' she said.

I took off my goggles and looked up at the sky. Bar the wisps of cloud it seemed pretty clear, though I had to admit the wind had got up.

'We've got thirty minutes, forty-five at most,' she said, sounding more resigned than worried.

Xander steered his sled around Tikaani's and let his dogs pull him a little way ahead. Then he moved to the side of the trail and deployed the drone, filming us as we drove our dogs towards him. After we had passed him, he pulled back into line, having programmed the drone to follow above us. I could imagine what his footage would be like: combined with my point-of-view stuff, I hoped it would be pretty epic.

Tikaani's weather forecast was, if anything, optimistic. Xander had not long brought the drone in when a thick cloudbank appeared on the horizon, and in minutes it had overtaken us. All shadows disappeared, the white expanse ahead flattening and foreshortening and filling with gauzy snowflakes, which seemed not to be falling from the sky but swirling up from the ground. We pushed on ahead, the dogs undeterred, as the flurry thickened, and we'd not been going long like that when I saw them.

Off to our left, no more than thirty metres away, dark figures loping between bushes that looked like scribbles in the snow. I yelled out to Tikaani ahead of me and the others behind, 'Look – wolves! To the left!'

Immediately, Tikaani's sled halted. I had to stamp on the bar brake to avoid running into her. Behind me, Caleb wasn't quite so quick: he veered off the trail to miss me. The others halted too.

'Did you see them?' I called out.

'Where?' Tikaani asked.

'Running alongside us. To our left.'

'Are you sure?'

'Yes!'

She had turned around to face me. Her expression wasn't disbelieving, more interested. 'Very rare,' she said, and at precisely that moment, behind her, the wolves crossed the trail.

I pointed, and she swivelled to look. We all saw them this time. Two, four, five, seven wolves, calmly trotting across the trail. The dogs saw them too. Tikaani's erupted in an excited rush of barking, which spread back down the line. The last wolf to cross stopped to look at them. It was huge and pale and, in the moment of its pausing, so still. After what seemed an age but was probably only five seconds it walked on again, looking completely unbothered.

'Is that, like, a problem?' asked Xander.

'I doubt it,' said Tikaani. 'They rarely approach humans.'

The snow fell harder as we got under way, and the visibility gradually worsened. Before long, we were hacking on through a proper whiteout. Tikaani's sled was just metres ahead of Brando and Dame, my lead dogs, but she kept flickering in and out of view. We'd been making good progress, with the dogs trotting at a steady ten or twelve kilometres an hour, and we'd been going for over three hours, so we had to be nearly there, surely? Now our progress slowed. The cold bit harder. I was exhausted. I was troubled too: I couldn't stop myself wondering whether the wolves had veered from our course, or were they alongside us, tracking us even? What did Tikaani's 'I doubt it' mean?

## 20.

In the whiteout, time seemed to stand still. Without being able to see the horizon ahead or trees flickering past, it was hard to believe that we were making progress. Yet eventually Tikaani made an abrupt left turn and not long afterwards, a shelter loomed ahead of us. It looked smaller than Tikaani's own cabin. After we'd fed the dogs – dry food this time – and tethered them on a bed of fresh straw in the lee of the hut (Tikaani assured us they'd slept out in worse conditions than this) I was relieved to step inside.

Caleb had some colour in his cheeks at last. He'd enjoyed the mushing, I could tell. It had invigorated him. He helped bring everyone else's kit inside, as well as his own, and offered to build a fire in the little stove. This was our only source of heat, for both warmth and cooking – or, rather, defrosting the blocks of stew Tikaani plonked unceremoniously in a big metal pan.

'Can anyone stay here?' Xander asked her.

'No. There are open wilderness huts dotted about Lapland,

but this one is privately owned. Mr Lukas reserved it.'

'It's quite basic,' said Amelia, hastily adding, 'I like it.'

She need not have worried about offending Tikaani, who replied, 'I'm glad someone does. It's better than nowhere. For a night it'll do.'

Darkness was already descending. When I glanced out of the uncurtained window, it seemed that the snow was easing up too. Caleb had volunteered to stir the thawing stew, so I listened to the quiet, which was broken only by the moaning of the wind and the sizzling of the frozen stew heating up.

Amelia sat down between Xander and me and said, 'I've been thinking,' her voice low.

'About?'

'The missing film, of course.'

The mention of it dropped a weight on my shoulders.

'It makes no sense for someone to have deleted it,' she said. 'For any number of reasons. For a start, you signed a non-disclosure agreement giving them the right to veto sharing it.'

'Just because you agree to something doesn't mean you have to stick to it,' Xander said.

'Fair enough. But deleting the film doesn't delete your memory of what went on in that room, does it?'

'Not everyone has a memory like yours,' I replied.

'True,' she conceded. 'But between the two of you, can't you piece together what you heard?'

Xander and I looked at one another. 'It was pretty boring, if I'm honest,' he said. 'Not a lot stuck.'

Amelia rolled her eyes. 'Boring on the surface, maybe. But

93

for someone to go to the trouble of deleting the recording suggests that something must have been said that, in the right – or wrong – hands, could be valuable. Talk me through what you can remember, at least.'

It didn't take that long. Amelia tried hard to hide her frustration, but when we got to the bit about the equations – which neither of us could remember that well – she puffed out her cheeks and shook her head. 'Unbelievable.'

'We thought we had them on the film though,' I said lamely.

'I know,' she said. 'But even so.'

We might have gone around in circles talking about it for longer, but we were interrupted by the dogs barking. It wasn't the excited yipping and yowling of the morning, but a cacophonous barking, signalling fury and alarm. Tikaani sprang from her seat in the corner, pulled a pistol from the top pocket of her backpack, and leapt outside. I followed her, Caleb close behind. We rounded the corner of the hut to find the dogs nearest us straining against their tethers, hackles up, barking for all they were worth. But the bigger commotion was at the far end of the line, where three enormous wolves had ripped a sled dog free of its leash and were tearing it apart.

# 21.

One of the wolves had the husky pinned down by the throat. Another was savaging its exposed belly. The dog's back legs were jabbing the air frantically as it tried – and failed – to kick the wolf away. The third wolf darted in, snarling and snapping at the poor husky's frenzied legs.

Tikaani raised the pistol but didn't fire it. Was she frightened of hitting the sled dog? That seemed absurd; in seconds the husky would be dead anyway if we couldn't drive the wolves away. But instead of shooting, Tikaani stared at the gun in disgust then threw it to one side. Clearly it wasn't working.

She snatched a log from the stack beneath the eaves and hurled it at the wolves. But she missed: the log fell short of the fight. I had better luck with the lump of wood I grabbed; I hit the wolf that had the dog pinned down, square on the back of its head. But my attempt was no more use than Tikaani's. The wolf didn't even look up.

I picked up a heavier chunk to throw as the third wolf darted in again. It took hold of the husky and dragged it – and the two other snarling wolves – backwards. Tikaani was still yelling and the sled dogs were barking as I drew back my arm to throw another log, but Caleb was suddenly in my way. Surging past me, he ran around the barking sled dogs and straight into the middle of the attack.

My cousin didn't have so much as a broomstick to hand. Unarmed, the best he could do was punch and kick. I couldn't believe his bravery. The wolves were fearsome, intent on one thing: killing the dog. And he was putting himself directly in their way. He was bellowing loudly enough to be heard over the cacophony, and he lashed out with a couple of well-aimed kicks, forcing the wolf savaging the husky's belly to slink backwards a couple of paces, if only for a second.

Next Caleb grabbed the wolf that had the dog by the neck. He kicked it and punched it and tried to rip the husky free. But as Tikaani and I ran to help him – I couldn't just stand there watching, and neither could she – he slipped and cried out. Suddenly all three wolves, a mass of bared teeth and flattened ears and raised hackles, had hold of the husky and were yanking it clear.

In an instant they'd dragged it ten, twenty, thirty metres away, well beyond the pool of light cast by the cabin. The dog was still screaming, but its cries faded as the wolves pulled it into the darkness.

The clamouring of the sled dogs quickly subsided, leaving an awful, hollow silence. The night seemed suddenly immense, the cold intense. Caleb, breathing heavily, was still on his knees in the snow, holding his left forearm against his chest with his right hand.

I knelt next to him. 'You OK?'

'That poor dog,' he said, rocking forwards and backwards.

Tikaani, having picked up the pistol, came across to us with it. 'Idiot,' she muttered. 'Idiot.'

'Did it jam?' I asked.

'No.'

'Is it out of bullets?'

'Again no. It's loaded all right. I am to blame. In my panic, I failed to undo the safety catch.'

Amelia and Xander were standing in the snow, Amelia wearing socks, and Xander framed in the doorway.

'They took Mikka,' Tikaani explained, shaking her head.

'I saw,' said Amelia. 'I'm sorry.'

I hadn't realised it was Mikka, Tikaani's prize lead dog, that the wolves had attacked; the half-light and the frenzy had obscured her. Seeing Tikaani with the dogs throughout the day, I knew how keenly she would have felt the loss of any one of them, but for it to have been Mikka was an added cruelty. As if to rub it in, the thin, high note of a wolf's howl welled up through the silence. Another wolf answered the first and, as we stood quietly, unable to comfort the guide, more wolves chimed in.

'How did they undo her chain?' Amelia asked.

I put my head in my hands. It was a good question, but now wasn't the moment.

Tikaani replied, 'They didn't undo it. The fixing was weak. I spotted it when I chained her up, and that's why I put her there. Of all the dogs, she would have been the least likely to stray.'

It struck me that if poor Mikka hadn't been tied up, she might at least have had a chance to make a run for it, but she'd been overpowered and unable to escape. I shuddered. Caleb looked ashen, as shocked as I was by what he'd witnessed.

'I'm so sorry, so sorry,' he kept repeating.

'It is not your fault,' Tikaani reassured him. 'If anything, it's mine. How stupid could I be with the gun?' She shook her head. 'You were brave; I am grateful. But I am also worried – are you hurt?'

Caleb had climbed to his feet, but he was still holding his arm in front of his chest. 'No, no. I'm fine. A scratch, I think.'

'Come inside. Let me look,' said Tikaani.

'What about the remaining dogs?' asked Amelia. 'Might the wolves return?'

'It is very rare for them to take a sled dog, or to approach humans at all,' Tikaani said. 'All I can think of is that their resources must be very low, leading them to attack out of desperation.' The guide's voice was quiet. 'But they have Mikka now; I doubt they'll return.'

'You doubted they would be a problem at all when Xander asked earlier,' Amelia pointed out. 'I suppose what I'm after is more of a sense of the probabilities involved.'

I put a hand on Tikaani's shoulder and said, 'Amelia cares. She really does.'

'I know,' the guide replied. To Amelia she said, 'If the wolves do return, the dogs will raise the alarm.'

'Yes, but by then it might already be too late,' Amelia

said. 'Going on experience to date, I mean. Also, we'll be slower to react if we're asleep.'

'Don't worry, I'll stay awake,' Tikaani said. 'And I'm not about to make the same mistake with the pistol's safety catch again.'

Xander stood to one side of the cabin's front door to let us guide Caleb inside. Following us in, he said, 'We can take turns to listen out.'

I nodded my agreement and was encouraged to see Xander do the same.

'Let's look at this scratch, then,' I said.

Caleb seemed reluctant to hold his arm out for inspection, and only did so when Tikaani gently prised it from his other hand. He was wearing a black wool base layer. When he took his fingers away, it was immediately apparent that the sleeve had been shredded. Blood ran thick and bright red through the sodden tear.

# 22.

'Some scratch,' said Amelia.

Tikaani sucked air through her teeth and said, 'You were bitten.'

'Seems so,' said Caleb. 'But really, it doesn't hurt.'

I doubted that. While Tikaani retrieved a medical kit from her pack I helped Caleb to take off the base layer, while he tried to keep pressure on the wound. The ripped sleeve was heavy with blood, which dripped from his fingertips.

'This will sting,' said the guide, holding a plastic bottle of clear fluid – alcohol, I assumed – up for Caleb to inspect. 'But we need to wash the wound before we close it.'

In fact, she meant 'wounds' plural. Whether it was a wolf or the desperate Mikka that had caught Caleb's arm, his skin had been punctured in five places, two of which were badly torn. I bit down hard in sympathy as Tikaani sluiced the cuts with alcohol, but to his credit Caleb barely flinched. She dabbed each cut repeatedly with a soaked pad of cotton wool, then closed the open wounds with steri-strips. Amelia explained that they were every bit as effective as stitches. That may have been true, but a little blood seeped through the butterfly plasters all the same.

'Here, hold this in place,' Tikaani said, wrapping gauze around Caleb's injured forearm. Her fingers were uncertain: she was no doctor, after all.

Caleb held the pad uncomplainingly, and waited patiently until Tikaani had finished wrapping the gauze around his arm. When she'd finished, she secured the dressing in place with two strips of orange duct tape.

'Compression will staunch the flow of blood,' Amelia said.

Caleb held his arm up, wagged it from side to side, and said, 'Good as new.'

Xander looked at me sceptically.

'I'll take the first watch, shall I?' Caleb went on. 'After we've eaten.'

'You should rest,' Xander said.

Caleb laughed. 'Why? I'm anything but tired.'

'We'll have to get you seen to in a hospital,' Tikaani said tentatively, adding, 'I suppose.'

'Er, yeah,' said Xander. 'You'll need –'

Caleb cut him off. 'What are you on about? I'm fine!'

There was a hint of the old defiance in his voice: I was happy to hear it.

'A dog bite can be a dangerous thing,' said Tikaani.

'That's what I was going to say,' Xander added patiently. 'When did you last have a tetanus jab?'

Caleb waved him away. 'Year or two back. Don't worry, I'm up to date. Anyway, Tikaani here has done a good job with the alcohol. I certainly felt that! The bite itself is nothing. I'm so, so sorry about Mikka,' he said to Tikaani. 'It's you who deserves sympathy, not me.'

Tikaani hadn't shed a tear about the dog and didn't look like she was about to crumple now. Her brusque, no-nonsense take on the world clearly extended to masking her grief. If anything, she seemed more distracted by sadness than overcome with it. 'Thank you,' she told Caleb. 'Mikka liked you.'

She could have said nothing better to help Caleb. The dog-sledding had brought him back to life – made him prepared to risk his life, in fact – and Tikaani's reminder of Mikka's affection for him, which we'd all witnessed, clearly meant something to him. He held up his bandaged arm again. 'With any luck I'll have a good scar to remember her by,' he said.

'I have painkillers if you need them,' Amelia offered.

Caleb shook his head insistently. 'No need. Forget about this. It'll heal up in no time. Let's just carry on.'

The old Caleb had an annoyingly stubborn streak, made worse by his arrogance. Now his stoicism about the bite felt selfless. He didn't want to make a fuss or be the centre of attention.

Xander refocused on the stew, which was bubbling in its pot on the stove. He and Amelia dished it out and we ate in silence. The stew was delicious and warming, laced with something that could have been paprika. Tikaani barely touched hers. Once the rest of us had eaten our fill she collected the pot, our bowls and spoons and took the lot outside 'to wash up'. I followed her to help. In fact, we rubbed everything clean with handfuls of snow before returning it all to dry on the stove-top.

The guide went through these motions with an underwater slowness. She was clearly in shock over her loss. It had shaken the certainty from her.

'You turn in too,' I said, when she suggested we get into our sleeping bags for the night. 'I'll keep watch to begin with. I couldn't sleep if I tried, not yet. I insist.'

Caleb and Xander said they'd sit up with me, but their offers somehow cancelled one another out.

'Thanks, but there's no point. Better if you both get some sleep.'

Tikaani and Amelia were already spreading their sleeping bags out on roll mats. Xander and Caleb did the same. They'd soon settled down, leaving me listening to the wind moaning through the trees outside. It was a plaintive sound.

I sat by the closed door, watching the orange flames through the glass stove-front. Its glow was the only source of light in the cabin. Amelia, lying nearest to me, was soon fast asleep with her mouth open. Shortly – it had been an exhausting day, after all – Caleb and Xander looked dead to the world too. I wasn't sure that Tikaani had – or indeed would – fall asleep that evening. She was lying on her side, her back to the room, facing the far wall.

Either way, I'd meant what I said: I felt electrically awake. So much so, in fact, that I found it hard to sit still. I decided to check the dogs, pulled on my snow boots and eased open the latch very slowly, making as little noise as I could. With a last glance inside I slid out, taking my coat with me. After the warmth of the cabin, the cold had a bracing loveliness to it, and the wind was a distant, unending oboe note, rising and falling. Those sensations will stay with me for ever, but what I saw that night outshone them all.

# 23.

The wind had dragged the sky clear of snow clouds, leaving a vast emptiness filled with stars, but the void was neither completely dark nor pricked with starlight: instead, it subtly pulsed with the Northern Lights.

I'd heard of this phenomenon, of course. Amelia had given us chapter and verse in the run-up to the trip. She'd told us its proper name was Aurora Borealis, explaining that the 'Aurora' bit referred to the Roman goddess of dawn, and that 'Borealis' differentiated the light show near the North Pole from the one over the South Pole, called Aurora Australis. She'd explained what causes the pulsing waves of light as well. It had something to do with electrically charged particles emitted by the sun entering the Earth's outer atmosphere and exciting the atoms up there, but I'd be lying if I said I understood the detail. The Earth's magnetosphere has something to do with it. As with many excellent and complicated things, the effect on me, as I stood beneath the pulsing sky, dwarfed the scientific explanation.

High in the sky, sheets of soft green light rippled and billowed, furling and unfurling, twisting and subsiding, gathering in intensity only to pour themselves away again. At times the greenness was pale, at times dark; for a while it was bluer, then it was tinged yellow again. I stood there with my head tipped back and my mouth open, amazed. As I watched, a deep red band flared along one edge of the green wave, flickered itself to a fullness, and rolled slowly across the starscape, only to be overrun with emerald again.

The hum of the wind through the trees, and its crisp coldness flowing over my upturned face, accompanied this phenomenal sight. I'm not sure how long I gaped at it, but the unknowable magic of what I was witnessing ran right through me like slow lightning, simultaneously blowing me apart and fusing me to the frozen ground.

I didn't wake the others. The moment was mine alone. If it connected me to anyone, it was to my dead brother, Mark. Like him, the lightshow was at once impossibly far away and yet within touching distance. It was mine and it belonged to nobody. I'd never fathom it, but it made complete sense.

I appreciate this sounds selfish, keeping the spectacle to myself, but a part of me reasoned that the Northern Lights, having shown themselves to me, would no doubt appear again the following night. I would tell the others and we could look out for them.

Finally, I walked around the cabin to where the dogs were sheltering, curled up, their tails over their faces, every one of them peacefully asleep and oblivious to the spectacle above. I hunkered down next to them, still watching the sky, which

106

kept up its magic into the small hours. Though I was out of the wind here, the cold crept through my layers, but instead of making me shiver it numbed me from within. I'm not religious and I don't know how to meditate or anything, but sheltering with dogs in the deep, dark cold beneath that incredible sky slowed me right down, making anything seem possible. Faith burned within me: Caleb would cope and we'd make it to the end of the trek and I'd find out Jonny Armfield's true identity and his connection to me.

I'd been out there a while before Tikaani appeared. She had her big parka on but it was flapping loose: she evidently wasn't planning on being outside for long. 'I woke to find you gone,' she said. 'You don't need to stay out here in the cold. I meant what I said. It's fine for us to rely on the dogs to raise the alarm if the wolves return.'

'But they're sleeping themselves.'

'Trust me, they're never that deeply asleep. Even resting like this, they're better at sensing danger than you and me. And we have the gun worked out now. It's my turn to listen out for them. Come back inside.'

I did as she asked, and I have to admit that I relished the warmth of the hut after the numbing coldness. Slotted into my sleeping bag, slowly warming up, I was soon overcome by a deep, peaceful sleep.

When I awoke, Caleb was already up and boiling water for coffee. I watched him out of the corner of my eye and was pleased to see him moving both arms freely. He'd already pulled on a fresh sweater: for a moment I couldn't work out which arm had been injured.

We opened the cabin door to let the day in and drank our coffee – black and scalding hot – beneath a sky so blue and sharp it looked like it had been Photoshopped. Following Tikaani's example, we wasted little time after feeding the dogs and eating our breakfast of nuts and honey, and we soon had everything packed up ready for the sleds. Before we set off, I overheard her asking Caleb again if he needed his wound looked at, and if he felt strong enough to carry on. He cut her off mid-sentence. 'I'm good to go. Let's get on with it!'

Nobody said anything about the loss of Mikka that morning, but I'm sure the others, like me, noted how subdued Tikaani was as she reconfigured the teams to account for the lead dog's absence. Before we set off, the guide gathered us to explain that the forty kilometres we had to travel that day would take us to the start of the second leg of our trek.

'This morning the dogs do much of the work; later you will make your way on foot with Kotler. It will be demanding,' she stated matter-of-factly.

'Who's he?' Amelia asked.

Tikaani didn't look up from the harness she was tightening. 'Another of Mr Lukas's contacts. We are headed for his facility now.'

## 24.

What 'facility' meant precisely, I didn't know. Tikaani set off without elaborating. I liked that she just expected us to follow. She'd also expected us to set up our own sled teams, although I knew she'd cast a subtle eye over our work.

The terrain the huskies pulled us through that morning changed as we went. Initially we were among big fir trees, their boughs heavy with fresh snow. But the trees gave way to thinner scrub that looked like iced tumbleweed, frozen in place. Our progress was slower to start with because Tikaani's team had to break the trail through the thick new blanket of snow. Soon, however, we'd arrived at a great flat expanse of hard-packed snow and we picked up speed, the sled runners beneath us hissing as we shot along.

We paused to take stock – and some film footage – at the far edge of this expanse, and Tikaani explained what should have been obvious to me: that we'd just crossed a sizeable frozen lake. Though the ice was thick – strong enough to drive a truck across, never mind a sled and dogs, she said – I felt nervous. The idea of falling through ice into freezing black water, and being carried away beneath a lake's glass lid, has always terrified me. I knew there could have been weak spots in the ice. If there were, Tikaani had steered us away from them.

Xander was quiet that morning. He had barely spoken as we ate breakfast and got ready to leave. His sled was ahead of mine. He didn't glance back my way once, or even seem to look around much; he kept his head down, his shoulders hunched and his eyes on the dogs ahead of him.

If it hadn't been for the missing film, I'd have guessed he'd fallen into a bit of a trance, and I would have understood why: it's pretty mesmerising watching the dogs bouncing on and on endlessly ahead of the sled.

But I guessed that he was worrying about the lost footage, doubting himself, perhaps – the most obvious reason for the file not being there was operator error, after all. I tried to take his mind off things when we stopped, and offered him some of the chocolate I'd squirrelled away in my pack, but he waved it away.

Beneath the bowl of the blue sky, drawn across the huge white canvas of the landscape by the sled dogs, we seemed to be heading off the edge of the map. But not long after our pit stop we pulled left onto what felt like a more established trail which, in time, turned into a snow road. I spotted the crenulated tracks of a snowmobile along it.

We were among gently rolling hills now. As we crested a rise, I made out a couple of low-slung buildings in the distance. This homestead, more substantial than any log cabin, turned out to be the place Tikaani had referred to as Kotler's facility.

We pulled up on a snowy forecourt and a man, as wide as he was tall, dressed in a huge fur-hooded coat and mittens, stepped from the bigger of the two buildings to meet us. Four more people followed him. They had an air of intent about them as they split up and came to relieve Amelia, Xander, Caleb and me of our sleds.

'Unpack your belongings,' Tikaani said. 'I'm returning the way we came with these guys. You're going on with Kotler here.' She turned to the broad man and introduced us briefly, quickly telling him about Caleb's injury and the loss of Mikka. Kotler took this information on board with a nod, and spread his arms by way of a welcome. The handover was a blur: I couldn't work out whether I was impressed or alarmed by the military speed of it. Either way, Tikaani, flanked by Kotler's assistants, was soon ready to depart with the sled dogs.

Before she moved off, Caleb walked the length of his team, reluctant to say goodbye to them, it seemed. The wheel dog, Storm, licked his ear as he knelt next to her. I noticed that he stroked all the dogs with his right hand, keeping his left arm close to his side. He didn't look pained by his injury so much as careful to protect it. Giving up the dogs was clearly a bigger issue for him.

As Tikaani, followed by the other teams, disappeared smartly down the snow road, Amelia spelled out what I'd been thinking. Turning to Kotler, she said simply, 'Well, that was a bit sudden. How do you fit into this trek then?'

'Like Tikaani, I've been engaged by Mr Lukas to give you a real Lapland test.'

'You mean taste?' Amelia said.

'No. Test,' he replied. 'Something that goes beyond the normal tourist experience. "Challenge the participants." That was my instruction.'

'Challenge us how?'

'To see what you are made of!' he said, no hint of a smile in his eyes.

'I'd say that Caleb has been tested pretty hard already,' muttered Xander.

'Yes, that was unfortunate,' Kotler replied with a shrug.

Caleb drew himself up tall and returned the gesture. 'Really, I'm fine, just sorry about the poor dog.'

'Most unfortunate,' Kotler repeated, immediately continuing, 'Now, grab your stuff and follow me.'

He gave us about thirty seconds to dump our kit in a plainly furnished dorm before calling us to assemble in what he called the briefing room. The dorm had been empty apart from a row of metal-framed beds, but the walls of this room were festooned with ropes and maps and racks of equipment, including ski poles, skis, and snowshoes. Kotler had taken off his massive coat and stood behind the big table in the middle of the room, his shirtsleeves rolled above his powerful forearms. The table had a glass top, beneath which lay a grey and white map.

'This afternoon we're heading into the hills here,' he said, jabbing a stubby forefinger into the middle of nowhere. 'It's a three-hour snowshoe hike. Our destination is a small lake. You're going to catch your dinner in it – I'll show you how – then hike back to cook it.'

'But it'll be dark well before then,' Amelia pointed out.

'I'll issue head torches if you don't have your own.'

'OK . . .' Amelia said, sounding sceptical.

'I'm up for it,' said Caleb, trying to inject some can-do into his tone.

'Great,' said Kotler matter-of-factly. 'Let's get kitted up.'

## 25.

The snowshoes Kotler gave us looked like the traditional ones I'd seen in films, but in fact they were a modern version of the same thing. They had the old-school hard-wood, torpedo-shaped frames, latticed with rawhide, but the bindings were made of nylon and the ratchet straps were plastic and metal. The snowshoes were bigger than I expected, nearly a metre long. Kotler explained we'd need this larger kind because much of our route would be through thick powder snow: the bigger the surface area of the snowshoe, the higher we'd float in the snow, making our progress easier.

He showed us how to position our feet in these ungainly contraptions – 'not too far forward or the hinged toe of your boot will snag when you raise your heel' – and he handed out hiking poles too. I'd always thought hiking poles looked pretty useless: the only people I'd ever seen using them were those daft power-walking types, strutting about on hills I could walk up perfectly well in trainers, but the poles proved useful in the snow that day.

There is a definite knack to walking in snowshoes. You have to exaggerate your movements, as if you're stepping over something with every stride, and you have to walk bow-legged so you don't tread on your own snowshoes. To begin with, as we marched out of the facility on relatively hard-packed snow, having torpedo-shaped tennis rackets strapped to my feet was a hindrance. But as soon as we struck out over the powder, they started to make an arduous sort of sense.

I knew the snow was deep – I could ram a hiking pole a fair way into it if I tried – but the snowshoes spread my weight so effectively that I only sank into it a couple of centimetres. Without them, the hike would have been an intolerable slog. With them, we'd surely cover the distance.

Kotler, leading the way, set a pace that started out brisk and got faster as the afternoon progressed. It was tough keeping up with him. We walked in single file, stomping on in his footsteps. Caleb, using just one walking pole, I noticed, was first in line. Then came Xander, then Amelia, with me bringing up the rear. I got into a rhythm, pumped the poles to stabilise myself, and pushed hard – as I could tell we all were, Caleb particularly – to match Kotler's stride.

Inevitably clouds overran the crystal-clear sky that afternoon, dropping gauzy, windblown snow, nothing like the whiteout of the day before but enough to bring the horizon close. The concentration it took to walk efficiently, the sheer effort of keeping up, and the reduced visibility had a numbing effect on me. Was that the point? Was Kotler – and by extension Armfield – dragging us out into the middle of nowhere to test our mettle, as he'd said, or was the trek a ploy to distract us, keep us out of the way? As I grew more exhausted, suspicions tormented me.

Ahead, a little distance had opened up between Caleb and Kotler. I was about to go past the others and ask if Caleb was OK when he sped up again, closing the gap. The same thing happened again a few minutes later. He was obviously struggling. I was too. Kotler forcing the pace like this felt almost malicious. I wanted to object, but I wanted us all to keep up more. He didn't deserve the satisfaction of breaking us. Would the invisible elastic between us snap before I did though? Just as I thought I was about to find out, the guide, his stocky silhouette just visible through the snow-laden trees ahead of us, stopped abruptly.

I drew up alongside Xander. He was breathing heavily. Amelia, whose swimming regime makes her the fittest of all of us, was bent double, gasping. And Caleb had sunk to his knees. The only satisfaction we had was the fact that Kotler was blowing hard too: in the dim late-afternoon light, his breath billowed from his nostrils in clouds of steam.

'Impressive,' he said. 'Now, it's time to catch dinner.'

I'd foolishly been expecting to see the lake once we'd arrived at it, but we'd emerged through the trees into this open area and were clearly standing on the edge of the lake's frozen, snowy surface.

Kotler, rummaging in his pack, said, 'Well done for keeping up. I wanted us to arrive before dark. It will be easier to show you what to do with a bit of natural light. Here – it won't be long before you need these.'

I waved away his offer of a head torch, pleased that I'd brought my own, and a little less angry with him for pushing the pace so hard: at least he'd had a reason to do so.

Next, he unstrapped two halves of a vicious-looking corkscrew-like tool from the side of his rucksack, slotted the segments together and held it out. 'This drill is called an ice auger. Modern ones are mechanised; this is much lighter, but a little harder work. Our first step is to make some holes.'

The wind had blown the snow on the lake's surface into drifts, so the plane of ice wasn't even dead flat. We followed Kotler out onto the expanse. I'm not sure I'd have guessed we were walking on a lake at all if I hadn't known. Kotler stopped and kicked a window of snow away from the ice with his snow boot. 'There are other ways of clearing the snow,' he said. 'Peeing on the ice brings good luck, for example. But in present company . . .'

Amelia turned to me. 'Is this guy for real?'

Kotler just laughed. 'Why do we clear the snow? Because fish are attracted to lighter areas where they can see better to hunt,' he said, setting the tip of the metre-long ice auger down in the middle of the snow window he'd cleared. 'This job can take a little while, depending on how thick the ice is.' Gripping the auger's pommel with one hand and the square section of its handle with the other, he slowly ground the tip of the wide corkscrew into the ice. As the blade bit and began to bore a hole, it spat out chippings of ice. Within a couple of minutes, he'd cut a hole fifty centimetres deep, through which he was able to plunge the shaft of the auger completely. Black water flooded up out of the hole. He worked more ice loose, reversing the auger back and to the surface.

'But look,' he said. 'There's still slush in the hole. If we leave it, the ice will quickly close over again.' He bent to retrieve a long-handled ladle – the sort you might use to dish up a casserole – from his pack and went on. 'So we use this to clear as much of the slush as possible.' He scooped out a few ladles full of gritty black ice and tossed it away. 'And once the hole is clear, we can fish.'

The rods he'd brought were stumpy little things. That made sense: there's no need to cast the bait when you're fishing straight down through the ice. Kotler showed us how to thread the silver and orange lures onto the line, and explained how the reel and brake worked. It was all pretty straightforward. We crouched near the ice hole as the guide dropped the lure through it and unspooled enough line for it to settle on the bottom.

'It's about fifteen metres deep here,' Kotler explained. 'Once the line goes slack, reel a little in. We want to fish near the bottom of the lake but not on it.'

'What exactly are we fishing for?' asked Amelia.

'Perch, grayling, possibly pike. Burbot, particularly at dusk. Maybe even an Arctic char.'

'Is there anything more to the technique?' I asked him, since simply sitting by a hole holding a stumpy rod seemed pretty basic.

'Not much,' Kotler replied. 'If you get no bites for a

minute or two, jig the lure up and down a metre or so. That'll give you something to do, and keep you a bit warm. But mainly ice fishing is about patience. We call it Finnish meditation. You,' he said, pointing at Caleb, 'you win this hole. I'll help the others set up at intervals across the ice.' He handed Xander the ice auger, shouldered his pack, and beckoned us on.

I'm not sure whether there was method in where Kotler chose for us to fish, but he spread us out quite widely. Each of us drilled and cleared our own holes. I was last and furthest from the rest. He'd brought tiny collapsible stools for us to sit on. Once my mini-rod and tackle were safely deployed, there was nothing for me to do but sit and do as the guide had instructed.

Quickly, the last of the light faded. I put on my head torch and sat over my glittery black hole in the ice, dipping and jerking my lure as darkness descended. The others were in their own pools of light. Was it really necessary for us to be so far apart? Again, my mind started playing tricks on me, cooking up conspiracies out of the cold and the dark.

And boy, was it next-level cold. I'd brought two extra layers in my backpack, plus a balaclava to wear under my beanie and fur-rimmed hood. I had inner gloves to beef up my mittens too. In the seconds it took me to pull this stuff on and climb back into my coat the cold dug its claws deep into me, and I had to do plenty of squats plus rod-jiggles to regain the lost body heat. I was famished, I realised: we'd set off from Kotler's place without eating any lunch. I was hungry, cold and – I admit it – a bit bored. Was this all part of the 'test'?

Minutes dragged by. No fish bit. My stomach rumbled. I looked at the sky. Cloud had snuffed out the stars and there was, I realised guiltily, no sign of the Northern Lights tonight. I still hadn't told the others I'd seen them. Pushing the thought away, I focused on the pool of torchlight in front of me, and the black hole at its centre, willing something to happen, and trying not to mind when it didn't.

Kotler had set himself up nearest to me, though still fifty or so metres away. The beam from his head torch, out of the corner of my eye, seemed unnaturally still. Xander's, Caleb's and Amelia's pools of light all moved more. Had Kotler mounted his light to something? Was he even there at all? Indeed he was; his light finally moved as he stood up to reel in a fish. Of course, he'd be the first to catch one. It stood to sod's-law reason. I stared down into my ice hole, trying to keep the beam from my head torch as still as his had been – maybe that was the secret?

And still I had no joy, fish-wise at least. I did notice something, however. By concentrating very hard for a long time on nothing but the hole, the shimmering blackness beneath it and the filament of my fishing line bisecting the two, the rest of the world – even, somehow, the cold and my hunger – faded away almost to nothing. The line became a point around which every other concern I might have rotated, at a vast distance. I was no longer bored, just calm, entirely in the moment, and incredibly focused.

# 26.

Caleb was the first of us to reel in a fish. The commotion he made, standing abruptly and winding in his line, startled me from my trance. Kotler had spread us out to work alone, but I decided to go and see what Caleb had caught – what was the worst the guide could do? I jogged over in my snow boots – the layer of snow on the ice made it easy enough to grip – and arrived at the same time as Amelia, who'd also decided to ignore the solo fishing advice, just in time to see Caleb yank whatever he'd snagged against the rim of his ice hole. The hook dislodged from the fish's mouth and the fish disappeared below the ice.

'I've read about that happening,' Amelia said. 'You're supposed to let the fish tire itself before pulling it up gently, nose first.'

'Useful to know,' I said. 'Better luck next time, eh Caleb?'

In the torchlight I couldn't tell whether he was smiling or grimacing.

'I guess,' he said, sounding a bit lacklustre.

'You've done better than the rest of us,' I said.

'Technically –' Amelia began, but stopped because Xander, who had jumped up from his stool, had clearly hooked a fish too. Rather than risk jinxing another catch, I stayed put this time. The three of us watched as Xander safely reeled in and landed whatever it was he'd caught. It didn't look particularly big from this distance.

'Perhaps they've decided to start biting,' I suggested.

'More like a coincidence, I reckon,' was Amelia's response.

'Worth giving it another go, anyway.'

She nodded her agreement. Caleb was already unspooling his line again. His movements seemed wooden, slow. Perhaps he was just being careful. I patted him on the shoulder, said, 'Keep it up,' and jogged back to my position to re-sink my lure. Now that I'd seen one of us succeed, it seemed all the more important to increase our collective chances of eating that evening by getting as many hooks in the water as possible.

Xander struck again next, followed by Kotler twice, then Amelia's whoop of joy told me that she'd also had some luck. But on the end of my line: nothing. Soon I was back in my Zen-like waiting state, and this time it seemed to go on for ever. Although I was aware of the others having some success, I was alone with my own lack of it for what felt like an aeon. Caleb caught something. Amelia caught another. More minutes passed. Any time now, surely, Kotler would call a halt, wouldn't he? We still had that huge snowshoe hike back to his base ahead of us . . .

Just as I was getting ready to give up, the rod bucked in

my hand. Its stubby tip jerked down, went weightless, then jerked down again. I barely moved, just waited, a statue above my hole in the ice, as the line went taut and slack repeatedly.

With one hand gripping the rod, I set the GoPro strapped over my hat to record: footage of ice-fishing success would surely cut well into a film on sustainability.

Whatever I'd hooked, when it pulled away from me, felt pretty substantial. I fought my urge to reel the fish in quickly. For a good three minutes I just let it pull left and right in the deep beneath me. Then I began to worry that the line, sawing against the icy edge of the hole, might fray, so I began to reel the fish in as gradually as I could. It was still thrashing away down there, meaning it had to be properly hooked, but I didn't want to take any chance of losing it as Caleb had done.

Soon the fish was visible, flashing darkly through the hole. There was its silvery tail, its side, its blunt head. For an instant it angled up towards me. I struck. With a flick of the rod, I had the fish up through the hole and on the ice, flapping in vain.

I have to admit, success – after all that waiting – felt good. It was a decent-sized fish, thirty-five to forty centimetres, with a green-brown back and dark stripes on its sides. It flapped weakly as I prised the hook from its upper jaw. A second pool of light swam over mine. I glanced up, expecting to see one of my friends, but it was Kotler looming over me.

'Xander,' he said.

I sighed. 'He's over there. I'm Jack, remember.'

'No, you've caught a zander. Or pikeperch, if you prefer. It's a small one – they can grow much bigger – but still, decent eating. Well done.'

This praise, even for 'a small one', meant a surprising amount, coming from Kotler.

'And just in time,' he went on. 'Now everyone has tasted success we can make the return journey. Feeling strong?'

'Strong enough,' I said, though in truth I felt anything but: my legs were as weak as string and my empty stomach was twisted with hunger.

'Good.' He banged his mittens together once: the sound was as loud as a car door clumping shut. Across the ice he shouted, 'Pack up, guys, and let's get going!'

# 27.

Although there was no deadline by which we had to make it back to Kotler's facility – we weren't racing the sun as we had been on the way to the lake – the guide still set a relentless pace. He'd instructed us to stay tight to one another behind him and focus the beams of our head torches on the snowshoe prints of the person in front, so that we might literally keep in step with one another, but at the speed he took off, that was harder than it sounded.

Caleb was suffering the worst. He was immediately in front of me this time, and I could tell he was exhausted. If you fail to pick your snowshoes up high enough, it's easy to catch the frame of the shoe in the snow, sending you reeling. We'd not been going long before poor Caleb took his first tumble. I called out to the others to stop, and to be fair Kotler immediately did, but he only gave Caleb seconds to get back in line before he set off again.

I had to fight my own battle to bring up the rear. My head was light with fatigue, my limbs were heavy, my stomach was hollowed out; I had absolutely nothing left in the tank. I've had to dig deep before. In Somalia, when we'd been trying to outrun Armfield and his men, I collapsed. But I'd been bitten by a snake while we tried to make our escape. Now I was simply trying to keep up in the snow, yet I felt similarly lightheaded to the point of delirium.

After some time, we stopped to drink some water. Kotler shone his torch beam in each of our faces, one by one. Caleb squinted back at him, wavering on his feet. Xander can normally be relied upon to lighten the moment, but he'd turned in on himself too, his arms folded and his head bowed. He clearly wasn't about to crack a joke for anyone. At least the look in Amelia's eye galvanised me: she had her Channel-swimming-race face on. 'Think you can crack me?' her raised chin said. 'Think again.'

I shone my own torch at Kotler's square jaw. Was he enjoying taking us to the limit? Though what I really wanted to do was curl up and sleep in the snow, I forced myself to say, 'Shall we crack on, then? I'm looking forward to eating what we've caught.'

'That's the spirit,' he said, and set off immediately.

It was probably for the best. We'd have seized up if we'd rested for long. And in fact, the second leg of the return journey seemed to pass more quickly than the first. The wind had swung around behind us, so it was no longer mocking us by blowing snow in our faces, and perhaps Kotler did ease up a fraction, making it easier for us to keep to his pace.

Eventually I spotted the orange dot of his facility's lights ahead. As we trudged on, I could make out the lamplit windows and the brighter white external light in the yard. Beneath the latter we prised ourselves free of our snowshoes. They felt about three times as heavy as when we'd put them on.

The cosy warmth and windless quiet of the main building were almost unbearably pleasant after spending so long outdoors. I could have slumped down on one of the sheepskin-covered chairs and slept there and then, despite my gnawing hunger, but Kotler insisted that we help him gut and prepare the fish.

'Do you need all of us to do it?' Xander asked innocently.

'Well –' Kotler began.

'Because I'm thinking . . .'

I know Xander well enough to detect when the warmth in his voice is fake.

'. . . that too many cooks spoil the broth and all that.'

Amelia interjected. 'He's right. Jack and I will help. Let Caleb and Xander rest.'

Perhaps because my cousin looked properly ashen, Kotler relented. 'Teamwork is all about the division of labour, you're right,' he said. He pointed at Amelia and me. 'I'll teach you two how to prepare the meal, and tomorrow you can pass on the knowledge to your friends.'

'Great,' Xander said mock-cheerfully. 'I noticed a router in the briefing room. Any chance I could have the Wi-Fi code?'

Kotler laughed. 'There isn't one. It's not as if any strangers are within range to use it.'

'You don't mind if I –'

Kotler waved him away absently.

Xander immediately retreated. Caleb, looking dead on his feet, followed him. At the big enamel sink in the kitchen area Kotler, using a knife as long as my forearm but as thin as my finger, demonstrated how to slit open the fish we'd caught – two grayling, five perch and my zander – hook out their oily guts, cut away their tails and heads and fins, and fillet the flesh from their xylophone-like skeletons.

No doubt about it, fish guts are pretty smelly. I took my time washing my hands with the bar of soap Kotler provided once we'd finished the gutting. What did Xander want with the Wi-Fi code just now? He was up to something: no doubt I'd find out what in time.

Preparing the food to cook had reignited my hunger. The glistening fillets, set on a big white plate, looked much smaller than the fish they'd come from, and certainly not enough to feed all five of us. Luckily Kotler had a sack of potatoes for us to cook along with the fish. We slathered these in butter and salt and wrapped them in tin foil, then set them straight on the open fire in the living area. Once they'd been in there for a good hour, we heated a skillet on the same coals and flash-fried the fillets in more melted butter until their outsides were a crispy gold.

'One of you fetch the others, the other help me plate up,' Kotler instructed.

I headed off to find Xander and Caleb. They were in the bunk room. Caleb, lying on his side in one of the lower bunks, had his back to the room. When I entered, he rolled over stiffly and did his best to lever himself up, using his good arm. His face was the colour of the whitewashed wall behind him. Xander, meanwhile, his face tinted blue behind his open laptop, didn't even look up when I said, 'Hungry?'

Caleb shivered. 'I suppose so.'

I repeated myself. 'We've been slaving to make a decent meal of the fish you caught out here – surely you want some?'

'Hmm,' Xander said, looking deep in concentration. 'Yeah, sure, just give me a minute.'

I was gobsmacked. Having been through the same day as I had, I'd imagined they'd both be as famished as I was.

Caleb followed me into the main area, where, on a rough plank table flanked by two long benches, our food sat steaming on plates. I immediately tucked in. Amelia did likewise. And Kotler, looking us over with a glint in his eye that might even have been pride, seemed to enjoy his portion as well. Caleb mumbled something about it being very tasty, but he seemed to have to fight down each mouthful.

Perhaps he was just too whacked to eat. Xander joined us eventually. He ate fast and thanked us for cooking, but I'd never seen him look so distracted. He was miles away. If I hadn't known him better, I'd probably have put it down to the fact that exhaustion can take many forms. But he seemed genuinely preoccupied. What was he thinking about? When Kotler left the table to fetch more potatoes, I whispered, 'What's up? Are you OK?'

He nodded briefly. 'Yeah, I just need to get back to my laptop. If what I've uncovered means what I think it does, you're not going to believe the stuff I've dug up on GreenSword Investments.'

# 28.

Once we'd finished eating, I offered to do the washing up, releasing Xander to continue his research. I desperately wanted to find out what he thought he'd found out but, to keep Kotler off our backs, we needed to draw a proper line under the day. Amelia and I made a good job of clearing up, thanking him for taking us ice fishing and showing us how to prepare and cook what we'd caught.

'You're welcome.' He shrugged. Something about the gesture made it clear he'd only done it because it was his job to do so. Just like Lukas and Tikaani, Kotler had a poker-faced coolness towards us.

I tried to engage him, saying, 'I know one thing for sure' once the last plate was on the slatted wooden drying rack.

'What's that?'

'I'll sleep well tonight.'

He gave another shrug.

'All that exercise, plus a belly full of fish and spuds.'

'Spuds?' he said.

'Colloquial English for potatoes,' said Amelia. 'Jack's right: we all need a rest after today. Even you must be tired, right?'

Kotler, looking nonplussed, waved us away with a tea towel. 'Get some sleep then. Tomorrow you will experience snowmobiling and learn how to construct an igloo,' he said.

We made our way to the bunk room to find that Caleb had already crashed out, curled on his side. He hadn't even bothered to climb into his sleeping bag, and didn't flinch when Amelia unfurled it and spread it over him. Xander barely looked up from his laptop as she did this.

'What's the score?' I asked him.

Still tapping away, he muttered, 'Just wait a sec.'

'More dark web stuff?' Amelia suggested.

'Um,' he said.

'I get it,' said Amelia. 'You're concentrating.'

The two of us sat beside him on his bed as he worked.

'What's the dark web?' I asked. 'I mean, I know it's a dodgy part of the internet. But what is it specifically?'

When Xander didn't reply, Amelia filled the silence. 'Think of it as concentric circles,' she explained. 'The internet encompasses a lot of stuff. The World Wide Web is a subset of it, made up of publicly searchable websites, also known as the surface web. Your standard search engines – Google, Bing, Yahoo and so on – trawl through all these surface sites and come up with results according to key words and search terms. At this level, everything is traceable. Search engines can track which sites you visit

131

and which pages you look at, for how long, etc. It's all in the open, like the information on the sites themselves – you just have to click on the link. There are also subscription services, which hide stuff behind paywalls, like newspaper articles, and they require a passcode. But that's still all accessible to anyone who's willing to pay. There's way more to the World Wide Web than just these bits though. There's loads of stuff behind paywalls, a more secretive side to the internet.'

'I know,' I said. 'The dark web.'

'Technically,' she corrected me, 'there are two levels. First the deep web, which is just sites that don't show up on normal search engines for one reason or another. Within the deep web there's the dark web, which is stuff that's deliberately been hidden.'

'What's it hidden for?'

'Lots of reasons,' Xander cut in. 'Some of which are despicable. Things like –'

'I can guess,' I cut him off.

'But governments and corporations also use the dark web to keep their communications private – both for national security and to prevent industrial espionage. The dark web works on anonymity: nobody knows for sure who's who and people switch identities all the time.'

'Sounds confusing.'

'It is, until you learn to interpret it. There are special browsers that can help with that. But compared to the surface web, the dark web is slow and difficult to navigate.'

'So, to recap, there's this dark corner of cyberspace –' I began.

'Hardly a corner. It's enormous. The dark web is estimated to be about 5,000 times bigger than the surface web. It's big business too. There are billions at stake. Much of it has to do with shady trading of drugs, weapons and dodgy information. But some of it is legit. The thing is, for every anonymiser, like TOR, for example –'

'TOR?'

'The Onion Router. So-called because it wraps up a user's identity in layers and layers of "relays", like onion skins, to conceal their location and usage. Somebody is always trying to come up with a way to pierce the layers and reveal what's actually going on. It's a constant battle.'

'And you're a soldier in it?'

'I wouldn't say that. I'm just . . . interested. You like maps in the real world, Jack. I like finding my way around in the virtual one. And it's lucky for you that I do.'

'Go on then, what have you found out?'

'You know how I said that the original leads, revealing Armfield's interest in GreenSword and the itinerary for his trip here with Finn Macmillan, dried up? I thought they'd probably got wind that they were being snooped on and re-encrypted everything, so they could carry on their conversation elsewhere under different aliases, but it looks as if it must just have been routine archiving.'

'How come?'

'Because in the time we've been away, the same traceable digital fingerprints have started cropping up all over the place again. And this time they're linked to more specific stuff.'

A scraping noise filtered in from elsewhere in the building: Kotler moving a chair on the floorboards or something. The reminder that we were not alone made Xander lower his voice as he went on. 'I've not intercepted anything from Armfield this time. But the addresses he was communicating with – and others linked to them – have been active. There's a lot of chatter about the Nordic next-generation power project – stuff we know about. The thing that caught my eye was some chat about something they call the disruption event. I don't know exactly what it refers to. It's like they're deliberately not spelling the thing out. But they refer to "operatives" tasked with "delivering the optimisable blow". Look.' He angled the laptop screen our way and scrolled through a series of screenshots showing messages to and from addresses with names like 3drE78?-+jkb@flss80.

'NNGPP obviously refers to the Nordic next-generation power project,' Xander explained. 'And here, I think DE is short for the disruption event this guy refers to in the previous message . . . here.'

I scanned the messages. There were reams of them, many of them full of indecipherable – to me – sets of numbers. 'What do you think these are all about?' I asked, pointing at some strings of digits.

'I'm not sure,' said Xander.

'And those sets of random words,' Amelia said. 'Tightrope. Schools.Baffle. Frivolity.Repetition.Escalates. Plus Kicky. Threaded.Protest and so on. Looks like gibberish, but it can't be. What on earth is that all about?'

The same scraping noise percolated through to us again. The noise made me pause while I was still staring at the strings of digits and words, and I found myself sitting back against the wall, arms crossed, a smile on my face.

'They're locations,' I whispered eventually.

'How on earth is 528028 184834 or Host.Again.Flies. a location?' Amelia said, then immediately said, 'Oh, I see.'

'I don't,' said Xander.

'The numbers are eastings and northings – coordinates. And the words are from the What3Words app,' I replied.

'OK,' said Xander. 'So they're exchanging locations. It will be easy enough to work out *where* they're talking about from them. Tougher to guess *what* they're expecting to happen there.'

'Armfield and Macmillan are here to negotiate investing in the building of new power infrastructure,' Amelia said. 'But "disruption event" doesn't exactly sound constructive.'

'Do any other words or phrases crop up more than once?' I asked.

'A few,' said Xander. 'Some of which we've heard before.' He scrolled through the messages. 'Here, for example, these guys are talking about the *Polar Flow*. That's the ship Armfield and Macmillan have chartered, right?'

'Yeah,' I said.

'Well, that's mentioned a few times. And there's one other word that crops up more than once in relation to the disruption event.' His fingers flashed around the keyboard typing in a search term, but he must have mistyped because he came up with no results at first.

I couldn't head off my impatience. As he was re-typing, I asked, 'What is it?'

'This,' he said, pointing at the screen. 'Shockwave.'

# 29.

Although the three of us had been as exhausted by the day as poor Caleb, we couldn't stop ourselves puzzling over the messages Xander had found. We made some headway with the locations. One was inside the Norwegian port of Hammerfest – where the *Polar Flow* was due to set off from. Another seemed to point to a nondescript stretch of coastline up in the Svalbard archipelago. A third location in the middle of the Barents Sea looked pretty random, but a fourth, also in the Barents Sea, turned out to be the coordinates for the Snøhvit natural gas field. All of this was consistent with the messages basically being about the Nordic next-generation power project stuff.

'A disruption event could mean anything,' said Amelia.

'It sounds sinister to me,' I said.

'Yeah, but businessmen love to talk a big game, making perfectly ordinary deal-making sound all military. Read the *Financial Times* – they're always banging on about war chests and fire sales, campaigns, hostile takeovers and battle plans. A disruption event could just be the launch of a new marketing slogan, for all we know.'

'Codename Shockwave,' I suggested.

'Perhaps.'

'What I want to know,' I went on, 'is why Armfield parked us in the literal middle of nowhere while he and shifty Finn Macmillan get down to the business that presumably makes sense of all these messages.'

'That's a bit harsh,' said Amelia. 'On the face of it, at least. He took you two to that introductory meeting. You admitted it was boring. He's organised for us to do something far more interesting than sit around in an office. As far as he knows, we're here to work on the On the Brink film project.'

'On the face of it,' I repeated. 'But dig down a little and you have to admit it's odd that the footage of that "boring" meeting has disappeared, and that we've been packed off out of sight of whatever else is going on. Plus, the trip seems to have been designed to wear us out.'

'How'd you mean?' Amelia asked.

'Exhausting training over long distances. Also, running into those wolves. I know it's daft, but do you think Tikaani could have crossed their path on purpose?'

Amelia snorted. I knew she was right: I was being paranoid.

'Never mind us, she'd never have put her dogs in danger,' said Xander, ever reasonable. 'And you know,' he sounded hesitant, 'it's possible that the missing film is my fault. I mean, I don't think it is. I was sure I checked the camera. But we'd just got off a flight and things happened pretty fast at the start of the meeting. I could have made a mistake.'

'Why are you mining the dark web for evidence that something dodgy is going on, then?' I couldn't help asking.

His voice dropped lower still. 'Because I want to be wrong. I was hoping I might come up with something to prove I'm not going mad.'

'That's fair enough,' said Amelia.

'What's our next step though?' I asked myself as much as them.

'I need more time,' said Xander. 'I'm getting somewhere, I think, but like I said, this stuff is so slow to navigate. I'll keep at it tonight –'

'But we're all knackered!' I said, stifling a yawn.

'We don't have much choice though, do we?' he replied. 'From what I gather, we're heading into the wilderness tomorrow on snowmobiles, and we're building igloos to sleep in tomorrow night. Which means no more Wi-Fi for two days. If I want to make progress, it has to be now.'

Xander worked on into the night. I stayed up with him for a bit, but watching somebody else key stuff into a computer – particularly when they don't seem to be getting anywhere – is even more boring than watching another person gaming, and although there are whole YouTube channels devoted to that, it's never been my bag. I'd rather do than watch.

No matter how hard I tried to keep my eyes open, they kept shutting. Amelia, having announced that it made no logical sense for us all to be more tired than necessary, climbed into her sleeping bag and was soon breathing the steady in and out of deep sleep. Xander, his eyes narrowed in concentration, muttered something to the effect that I should follow suit. I didn't like to leave him to it but, given the uncertainty of what we'd be facing the next day, that's what I did, and I swear I fell asleep before I'd even pulled up the zip on my sleeping bag.

# 30.

I woke before the others, thirsty as anything; Kotler had cooked dinner with a lot of salt. Careful not to wake anyone, I headed to the kitchen to grab a glass of water. Outside, dawn was breaking. Something was moving within the open door of the shed opposite. Curious, I took a step closer to the window, just in time to spot Kotler dragging a small orange box across the shed. Whatever was in it seemed heavy. As he bent to lift it, he looked up and saw me framed in the window. I couldn't make out his expression, but he immediately hefted the box out of sight. There was something furtive about the way he did this: his body language suggested I'd caught him in the act – of doing what, I had no idea.

I retreated to our room to find Caleb awake and shivering.

'How are you doing?' I asked him.

'I'm all right, but I admit I'm not up to snowmobiling. I've been thinking: we could turn it to our advantage. Tell Kotler that Xander should stay behind with me.'

Over breakfast of pancakes, bacon and syrup, which Caleb didn't get up for, we persuaded Kotler – who didn't mention having spotted me in the window – that leaving the two behind was the best plan. Xander had spent much of the night on his computer, he said, getting nowhere. He did a good job of looking genuinely disappointed to miss out, though the bags under his eyes told me that he was almost as exhausted as my cousin.

I half expected Kotler to object: the day before, he'd seemed determined to push us on at all costs. But he didn't. Perhaps he thought he'd already broken Caleb and Xander. In which case, job done. With another of his dismissive shrugs he said, 'Mr Lukas wouldn't forgive me for truncating the trip entirely.' Nodding at me and Amelia, he went on, 'It's safest to take the two of you out. At least I'll have done my part of the deal if I do that.'

While Amelia and I gathered our gear, I thought about Kotler's use of the word 'safest'. Did he mean that letting Xander stay with Caleb would keep everyone safe, or that he needed to take some of us out as planned to be safe from the repercussions of disobeying Lukas's orders? Surely the former. Kotler was no pushover. How could Lukas be that much of a threat to him? When I raised this with Xander, he opened his laptop and said, 'See if Kotler will tell you any more about Lukas and Armfield when you're out and about. I'll carry on searching with this.'

Back in the yard, Kotler was in his element again. He'd already set out three orange and black snowmobiles. Once he'd issued us with properly fitting helmets – mine even

142

had a GoPro mount, which would make it easy for me to film the day's exploits – he walked us around one of the machines, explaining how it worked.

Basically, they have a Kevlar caterpillar track towards the rear on their underside. Open up the throttle and the track spins backwards, propelling the machine forward. You use the handlebars to turn the skis on the front to steer, and your body weight to shift its centre of gravity. As he was telling us to keep one finger on the brake lever at all times, it occurred to me that snowmobiling might be a bit like mountain biking, and although there were obvious differences I was more or less right.

For starters, piloting the snowmobile was all about body position. In anything other than bog-standard conditions you don't just sit down on it, and you don't stand up stiff-legged either. Like mountain biking, you take a sort of bent-kneed attack position, from which you can shift your weight forward and back as the terrain dictates.

As soon as we got off the track and into deeper snow, it became clear that piloting the machine was all about conserving momentum. To do that properly I had to pick a line and set the machine up for it. Staring down at the skis was as pointless as staring at the front wheel of my bike. But if I looked ahead and blipped the throttle or brake at the right time, I could help the snowmobile surf up banks and steer round obstacles. Of course, there were big differences. The main one was that on a snowmobile you sometimes have to position yourself all the way to one side of it or the other – the equivalent of standing on one mountain-bike pedal with the wrong foot. The running boards on a snowmobile are bigger and easier to stand on though, and when you're traversing a slope, you have to yank the machine up onto one ski by standing on one side of it and leaning it right over.

Kotler showed us how to do all this, expecting us to keep up. He took us north-east, into a rolling landscape full of trees, slopes and deep snow, and although we got the hang of piloting the machines pretty quickly, we also got stuck more than once. It didn't matter; he taught us how to rock, yank, roll, dig, turn and break our snowmobiles free of clagged snow. By lunchtime we were even surfing up banks and over mounds, looking for airtime. Although the snowmobile weighed about ten times as much as my bike, the weightlessness of jumping it felt very similar. I came close to crashing the thing a couple of times, but Kotler didn't look worried.

Although I had no map, my sense of direction told me we were taking a circuitous route on the snowmobiles. Kotler was navigating the landscape to teach us how to drive the machines, rather than just cover ground on them. After a lunch of hot vegetable soup, which Kotler poured from a battered thermos, he dug deeper into his backpack and came up with a sheathed saw, a folding shovel and a ball of twine.

'With these we can make the best of all snow shelters,' he said. 'An igloo is sturdier and warmer than a tent. There's a knack to building them though. Mr Lukas has asked me to teach you.'

'How do you know him?' I asked innocently.

'We go way back,' he replied. 'I've done a lot of this type of thing' – he waved the saw in the general direction of the snowmobiles – 'for him.'

'That's not really an answer, is it?' said Amelia.

For a second, I worried that her combative tone might annoy Kotler, but he ignored it. 'You're right. In fact, we were in the military together many years ago. That's where I learned many of the survival skills I now pass on to clients.'

'Did you come across a guy called Jonny Armfield in your time soldiering?' I couldn't help asking this question. It just came out.

'Jonny. Oh yes. He, Lukas and I got ourselves into – and out of – many scrapes together back in the day.'

'Scrapes?'

'They came with the territory.' He shrugged. 'But now my work is with civilians. Like his, I think?'

Kotler didn't blink or sound cagey at revealing this connection; he obviously didn't think he was giving anything away. This reassured me somehow. Armfield was using his connections to do what he'd promised: show us the real Arctic wilderness. That had to be a good sign, didn't it?

# 31.

Kotler was already moving on. He'd tied one end of the twine to the shovel as he was speaking and now jammed the blade into the ground. Having reeled off a length of twine, he tied a stick to it. 'First, we mark out the footprint. For a two-man igloo, a radius of two metres is more than sufficient.'

'But there are three of us,' Amelia pointed out.

'There are now, but there won't be tonight,' he replied.

Using the tethered stick, Kotler marked out a circle in the snow. Then he handed me a shovel. 'First of all, clear all the freshly fallen surface snow. Dig down until you hit the firm stuff below.'

Taking turns, we started to dig out the frothy, loose snow within the circle. It was about half a metre deep. Once we'd shovelled it all beyond the perimeter Kotler took the shovel from Amelia. 'Now we're down to the firm crust, we dig deeper. First, a narrow pit to stand in.' He dug this hole himself in under a minute, cutting out a

146

neat, square-sided, waist-deep pit. 'The deeper we go, the lower our walls need to be,' he explained.

'How do we build them?' Amelia asked.

'With blocks cut from this stuff,' he said. 'Pass me the saw, please.'

I handed him the saw and we watched as he cut a rectangular block about seventy-five centimetres long, forty centimetres wide and thirty centimetres deep from the side of the hole he was standing in. He had to kneel down to cut the base of the block free. Once he'd done this, he eased the block out of its slot and lifted it clear. 'Easy, eh?'

He'd made it look so, but I doubted it was. Nevertheless, having made just the one example he jumped out of the pit, gave me the saw, pointed at his perfect block and said, 'Start by cutting as many of these as you can from inside the circle. I'll be back in a bit.' With that, he shouldered his pack and walked off into the trees.

'Okaaay,' said Amelia, watching him go.

After transferred the GoPro to a chest mount and setting it to film the build process, I jumped into the hole with the saw and copied Kotler. The saw cut through the snow ridiculously easily. I used the gap Kotler had left to cut a block I thought would be the same size, but my first attempt broke in half as I tried to lever it free. I managed to lift the second one to waist height before it too broke in half. The slot I was working in had been a neat rectangular hole, but now it was full of loose snow. Impatience rose within me.

'Go a bit slower, perhaps,' Amelia suggested.

'Thanks,' I said. 'Hand me the shovel. I'll clear this lot and start again.'

Although her advice did little to calm me, once I'd tidied up the hole I tried to do as she suggested and cut the next block super-methodically. It worked. I'd made a single block and felt pretty good about it. A corner broke off the one after that, but soon I was making more successful blocks than broken ones. Those that worked, we stood on end like crenelations around the ever-expanding pit.

Amelia must have been watching me very closely as she seemed to have learned from my mistakes: the very first block she made was a success. We took it in turns to make more and more, and by the time Kotler got back – he never said where he'd been – we'd more or less cleared the inside of the circle and made thirty or so viable building blocks in the process.

'It's a start,' he said, smacking his mittens together. 'But you have to work faster. You'll need to cut another pit at a distance to dig more blocks from in due course, but let me show you what to do with these ones first.'

With that he jumped down into the now circular hole, scraped the floor level, and firmed up the floor and the walls of the pit with the back of the shovel. When he was satisfied, he performed the same levelling-and-tamping-down job on the rim of the pit, making a sound surface on which to lay the first ring of blocks.

Before he set the first block in place Kotler took a length of twine and pegged it in the dead centre of the pit, checking that he'd found the right spot by using the twine to measure the radius of the circle, tracing the hole's circumference. With the twine securely in place, he set the first block lengthways on the rim of the pit. He butted the second block up against it. 'It's very important that the joints between the blocks point directly at the centre of the circle.' Using the saw in line with the taut twine, he feather-cut the joint between the two blocks. 'If you do it like this, the twine acts as a failsafe spoke, pointing the way to the hub of the igloo.'

The twine came in handy for the next step of the building process as well. Once Kotler had laid an entire ring (Amelia and I worked together to set the last block in it), he bevelled off the top of all but one of the blocks in the ring at an angle pointing down to the igloo's hub, using the saw as an extension of the taut twine. The one block he'd left proud became the anchor point for the first block in the next layer, all of which were angled inwards a little because we were setting them on a now bevelled edge. Kotler got us to lay this second layer ourselves, only intervening with puffs of exasperation to correct obvious mistakes – which were, I admit, numerous.

'I can see a problem with this,' Amelia said as we finished the second layer.

'What?' I asked.

'We've built a sloping wall around ourselves. How do we get out?'

Kotler shook his head as if the question was idiotic. 'We need to climb out now anyway, both to strengthen the wall from outside and to cut new blocks for it. So, we dig the entrance.' He did this carefully, cutting a hole at floor height – well beneath the rings of blocks we'd built – and creating an angled slope up to the surface outside the wall. When the tunnel was big enough to crawl up, that's what he did. We followed him out. Once we were all at ground level outside the shelter, we helped him enlarge the chute entrance and strengthen the block wall from the outside.

'Every time you finish a layer, you have to cram snow wedges into the external gaps,' Kotler explained, doing just that. 'The wedges act as a sort of bonding cement, making the structure sturdier.'

With the gaps plugged, we cut more blocks from a new hole twenty or so metres away and carried them back to the half-built igloo. Working together, from without and within, we sped up the process of laying the igloo's further block-rings. But as the angle of the blocks tilted further and further inwards, they seemed ever likelier to fall in.

'Give a little support here, and here,' Kotler indicated. 'On my own, I'd use walking poles as props if necessary, but since you're here I'll use you.' With us both helping to support the penultimate ring he went on: 'To make a perfect dome, the top of each block-ring should be exactly one cord's length from the hub.'

Testing this proved it to be the case.

'Now,' he said softly, 'when the hole in the dome is shoulder-wide, we lock the whole thing together using a capping block, like so.' He delicately posted the last block up through the hole, turned it on its side and sawed off its edges from below, easing it back into the opening. 'You can stop propping once it's safely in place,' he said, cutting the block flush into the gap. 'Gravity is working for us now, pulling the whole thing together, compressing the dome down onto that final capping block. Unless something shakes the structure, it will hold itself in place.'

Kotler's 'unless' sounded ominous to me. A bear, an earth tremor? The thought of being buried under those blocks of snow sent a shiver right through me.

Without pausing to admire our handiwork, he went on. 'We're not done yet though. Follow me outside.'

To finish the igloo, we plugged every last gap between the blocks, both strengthening the shelter and windproofing it.

'And we need to complete the entrance tunnel,' he said, 'by giving it a pitched roof. That's easy – just lean two blocks together tepee-style, and extend it with another couple, like this.'

We threw a layer of fresh snow over the entire igloo as a finishing touch, then Kotler retreated to his snowmobile to fetch supplies. Standing back to survey our work, I noticed that the light was already fading. It had taken us longer than I'd realised to build the igloo, and the piercing blue sky we'd worked beneath was a thin, purplish colour now. If it stayed clear I might yet have a chance of showing Amelia the Northern Lights . . .

The supplies Kotler had mentioned included inflatable, rubber-backed sleeping mats and our heavy-duty four-season sleeping bags. He'd also brought a frozen block of what he casually described as 'reindeer stew'.

'It's pretty much the national dish,' Amelia explained.

'And you should taste the national drink as well,' Kotler said, pulling a bottle full of a clear liquid from his pack.

'What is it?'

'Vodka.'

'I'm all right, thanks,' I said.

'Me too,' said Amelia, waving away the offer. 'I've never understood the allure of alcohol. Why deliberately make yourself more stupid?'

Kotler sneered. 'It's bad luck not toasting a new house, but suit yourselves.' With the air of a man proving a point, he raised the bottle and took a swig. Then he wiped his mouth. 'You have shelter, the number-one priority for survival. There's dead wood around you can use for a fire. You also have food, and if your water bottles run dry, out there's enough of the stuff frozen all around you to melt and drink. It's just one night. I'll return in the morning. You can't make a mess of it.'

He seemed to imply the opposite, but he didn't add more or even look back as he roared off into the gloom.

## 32.

Although night was falling it was still way too early to go to bed, so we set off into a nearby stand of firs to gather firewood. I took the shovel, and we soon uncovered enough dead branches and fallen twigs to start a fire. As I was in the process of clearing the ground – to lay the kindling upon – Amelia stopped me.

'You've obviously not read the Jack London story *To Build a Fire*, have you?'

'Er, no.'

'Well, in it this guy, who's trekking in the Alaskan wilderness with his dog, accidentally steps into a stream. It's forty or fifty degrees below zero. His soaking fur boots immediately freeze. He has one chance to build a fire, thaw and dry out his boots, and warm his feet. He knows that if he doesn't manage this immediately, the cold will incapacitate him and he'll die. So he acts quickly. Gathers wood like we have. Plonks it down and sets it alight. Look up.'

I did as she said. Spread out above me were branches freighted with snow. 'Ah,' I said.

'You get it?'

'I do.'

'Well, the guy in the story doesn't. He sets his fire going all right and just as he's congratulating himself for having averted a disaster the snow in the branches above him melts and a lump of it falls on the fire, putting it out. He doesn't have enough time to make another one. He looks at his dog. It knows the score and sets off to find shelter, leaving him there – spoiler alert – to die.'

Something about Amelia's straight-up delivery made me laugh. 'Nice dog.'

'It acts on instinct. That's the point of the story, really. The man thinks he's clever enough to outwit nature, but the dog's instinct for self-preservation is stronger.'

I moved out from under the tree canopy. 'Well, we're not quite in a life-and-death situation here, thankfully, but I'll start the fire out in the open anyway.'

Much of the wood was dry and snappable, which made lighting it easy. We soon had a crackling fire going. The bright orange tongues of flame immediately made everything beyond seem properly dark, so I set off to retrieve our head torches before night closed in on us. I brought the pan of reindeer stew and our metal plates and forks. The fire would heat it just as well as any stove.

We passed the time hunkered down next to the fire or scrabbling around with our head torches looking for more firewood. The reindeer stew tasted, unsurprisingly, a bit like venison. Sitting back after I'd eaten my second helping, I noticed that the vault of darkness above us was now studded with stars. They seemed almost close enough to touch.

Would the Aurora Borealis show up again? I wondered. Sadly, no. Though we stayed out a few hours, the phenomenal light show didn't happen that evening. I was tempted to admit to Amelia that I'd seen it already, but I held back. We didn't chat much about anything, in fact. When you've known somebody your entire life, you can be comfortable sitting in silence.

Eventually it was time to go to bed. We let the fire putter out and made our way back to the igloo. We leopard-crawled through the entrance tunnel and, once inside, plugged the hole up with our packs. I took off my snow boots, gloves and parka but wriggled into my sleeping bag wearing everything else, including my beanie. I filmed all this on the GoPro, and got some mental footage of the beams from our head torches scissoring about wildly as we sorted ourselves out.

When we extinguished them, I was surprised not to be plunged into total darkness. There was enough ambient light outside to filter through the blocks of snow. I couldn't exactly see by it, but the igloo wasn't pitch black. Although we'd flung a layer of snow over the blocks, I could still make out the lines where they joined: it was like looking at a brick wall with my eyes almost shut.

The air in the igloo was cold, obviously, but there was no wind to cut through it. Cocooned in my sleeping bag, I was warm enough. I lay still, breathing slowly, trying not to think about what else might be out there, and just about succeeding. But a while after we'd settled into our top-to-toe sleeping bags, just as I was about to fall asleep, Amelia broke the silence.

'I know why you need to work out if Armfield is for real,' she muttered. 'As in I actually get it.'

'I know you do,' I said.

## 33.

I slept without dreaming, clean through the night. Next thing I knew, the igloo's walls were electric blue, the joins between the bricks a bright white. I checked my phone. It was quarter past nine. The sun had been up a good hour and a half. Seeing that my phone's battery was below ten per cent, I switched it off to conserve power.

Beside me, Amelia had pulled the hood of her sleeping bag so tight that only her nose and mouth were visible, but it turned out she was awake. When I unzipped my own bag she said, 'Ah, finally,' and wriggled the hood open from within.

'We should pack our stuff. Kotler could be here any minute.'

'I was thinking the same thing.'

We broke camp. It was a bright, clear day. Still, almost windless, and eerily quiet. We would hear Kotler's snowmobile, when he arrived, from a distance. I made another fire and scooped snow into a saucepan to melt over it. The provisions Kotler had left for us included a jar of coffee, so we made black coffee.

Perhaps the coffee was too strong; it certainly made me want to get on with the day even more than usual. We washed up with snow, put everything away and sat on our packs, waiting for Kotler to show up. Ten o'clock came and went. I banked up the fire, as much to give myself something to do as to ward off the cold. It was much easier to find firewood in the daylight: the fire was soon a big one, its flames flickering head-high.

Neither of us wanted to say it out loud, but as eleven o'clock slid by I couldn't help myself. 'Where the hell is he, do you think?'

'Technically there are still fifty-two minutes of morning left,' Amelia replied.

'Yes, but I kind of expected him here first thing.'

Amelia shrugged half-heartedly. 'Then you expected wrong.'

North of us – the way from which we'd come – the open snowfield rose gradually in a smooth incline. Pointing that way, I said, 'I'm going to head up to the ridge and watch for him coming.'

'I can't see much point in that,' Amelia said.

'It's something to do, at least. I'm no fan of waiting.'

'If it makes you feel better, fine. No need for us to lug everything up there though. I'll wait here with the stuff.'

I set off. The ridgeline wasn't far. As I crested it, the expansive plain we'd crossed the day before spread itself out before me, a huge white tablecloth of snow stretched taut across the land. Apart from a few birds flapping lazily overhead, nothing in the scene was moving. I squatted on my heels, squinted at the horizon and waited.

Amelia was only a few hundred metres away but I felt very alone, marooned in that huge expanse of white. The minutes ticked by. Once I felt sure that midday had passed, I fired up my phone again, relieved to see that, though the battery was low, it had a bar of signal. I called Xander. 'Is Kotler with you?' I asked when he picked up.

'No.'

'What time did he leave?'

'What are you talking about? He left with you.'

'Didn't he return last night?'

'No.'

I cut across whatever Xander was about to say. 'About to run out of juice – I'll see you later.' I ended the call and switched off my phone, sliding it into my pocket. I stood up and put my hands on my hips. Kotler hadn't just missed his deadline. For some reason I couldn't explain, I knew he would not be returning at all.

## 34.

I trudged back down the slope, clear about what we had to do, but fearing that Amelia would take some convincing. But she'd reached the same conclusion as I had.

'Do you reckon you can navigate us back alone?' she asked when I reached her.

'Yes,' I said, doing my best to sound more certain than I actually felt. 'And we should get going now, for two reasons.'

'To maximise daylight,' Amelia said.

'Yeah, and the other is snowfall. Or lack of it. The snowmobile tracks are still visible – for now. The fact that it's not been windy should also help; our tracks won't have been covered by windblown drifts.'

Kotler had brought much of the equipment – our packs, shovels, bedding and provisions – on a sled he had pulled behind his snowmobile. We had to decide what to take back with us, and what to leave for him to pick up later. We could cram some of the stuff into our packs but – I worried aloud – would we be able to pilot the snowmobiles properly, weighed down like that?

'We don't have much choice,' Amelia reasoned. 'If we get lost and have to spend the night outside, we'll need all that gear to keep us alive.'

She was right, but still . . . Just climbing onto the snowmobile wearing the pack was awkward, never mind negotiating any tricky obstacles with it on.

'Let's take it slowly,' I said before we started the snowmobiles. 'If we stay well within our limits, we'll be all right.'

Following the tracks was easy enough to begin with. Kotler had retraced the last part of our route so there were multiple, easily spottable tracks over the same ground. We soon crossed the first expanse and made it into hillier terrain. But among that stubby, snow-enveloped scrub, we came to an apparent fork in the trail. I slowed to a halt, cut the engine, and waited for Amelia to do the same behind me.

'Those are our tracks, heading that way,' I said, pointing. 'We crisscrossed each other, coming in from the south-east. But Kotler evidently cut due south here, see? One set of tracks heads that way.'

'Presenting us with a dilemma.'

'Yeah. It'll be easier to follow our multiple tracks . . .'

'But we came via a circuitous route. Kotler was showing us how to handle these things' – I tapped the snowmobile's handlebars – 'in different types of terrain. He'll have headed back the quickest way, I reckon.'

'You'd think,' said Amelia.

'You sound sceptical.'

'Well, I didn't say anything at the time, but he drank that vodka before he set off. He could have deviated . . . unintentionally.'

'I doubt that,' I said. 'It looked like he was used to it. I say we go the way he went. If we hit a problem, we can always come back to this point and pick up our trail.'

Amelia adjusted her helmet, shrugged and nodded, and we carried on our way.

Kotler's return trip cut through sparse woodland. He'd woven through the trees, heading gently downhill, before picking up a path that wound its way between low-lying hills. I'd been following this open stretch a good few minutes before I realised it was a frozen stream. The going was easy, level, a series of gentle curves that soon joined another tributary and broadened into a bigger river. Kotler's tracks hugged the left-hand bank for a mile or so. Then the river swung lazily to the south-west and opened out further into what had to be a lake. The tracks made by Kotler's snowmobile set out straight across it, then gradually veered to the east.

I was tempted to open up the throttle as we followed his route across this expanse, but something stopped me. It was the colour of the snow ahead: the bright white immediately in front of us softened to a weird grey. In fact, fifty or so metres away, closer to the far shore than the one behind me, it looked like there was an abrupt strip of . . . black.

I brought the snowmobile to a halt and motioned for Amelia to follow suit.

'Something's not right,' I said, setting my pack down on the seat of the snowmobile. 'Look.' I pointed. 'What's that?'

Amelia narrowed her eyes. 'Oh my God.'

I set the GoPro to record and took a step forward.

Amelia put her hand on my arm. 'Wait. If we're going to do that, let's do it like this,' she said, lowering herself to all fours. 'To spread our weight.'

I dropped to my hands and knees beside her, and we crawled across the grey ice. We covered the ground slowly, following the snowmobile's tracks. I was hoping against hope that they would change course, but they headed straight towards the black hole ahead. Amelia spelled things out as we went. 'He was travelling in the dark. The snowmobile's headlights tinge everything yellow. And he'd been drinking. He could well have cut straight across this without seeing the colour change.'

'But why would one bit of the lake ice be thinner than the rest?' I asked.

'It could be a thermal current of some sort, a spring,' said Amelia.

'Surely he'd have known about it?'

'You'd have thought, but although it's not exactly warm, it's usually colder than this here. Maybe the ice is unusually thin. Hold on. Shh.'

We halted. The silence felt huge, but actually it was underscored by a faint hum, a bit like the kind you hear if you stand near an electricity pylon. The ice seemed to be singing beneath our weight. By now we were only eight or so metres from the hole. Dropping to my belly, I leopard-crawled another three or four metres. The snowmobile's tracks ploughed straight into the shimmering black water. Another metre on, I levered myself up on my hands, and saw a flash of orange deep beneath the surface.

'I can see it,' I said.

'What?'

'The snowmobile,' I said. 'But there's no sign of Kotler. He could have clawed himself free.'

'He wouldn't have tried that,' said Amelia.

I swivelled to face her. 'Why not?'

'Clawing at the edge of the ice just risks breaking more of it off. You have to kick your legs up behind you and keep kicking, pulling with your arms if you can, sort of swimming yourself up onto the ice, staying as flat as possible the whole time. Then once you're onto firm ice, you roll away from the hole. Can you see any drag marks?'

I looked left and right, but couldn't see any sign that Kotler had pulled himself to safety.

'Look for pick holes,' she added. 'Snowmobilers sometimes carry little screwdriver-like picks – you can even get them to wear around your neck. They use them to jab into the ice and get a hold on it. He could have had some on him. If you know you're going to be snowmobiling over thin ice, they're a worthwhile precaution . . .'

I know Amelia well; she was trying to make herself feel better with this knowledge, avoiding thinking about what actually seemed to have happened to Kotler. I searched for any pick-marks in the ice but found none, and told her so.

'Come away from the edge then.' There was resignation in her voice.

Gingerly, with the ice creaking and the full horror of Kotler's accident sinking in, I slid away from the hole.

## 35.

'We need to mark this location,' I said, reaching for my phone. It had just three per cent of battery life left when I turned it on, which meant it could die at any time. Working quickly, I opened the What3Words app and read the three words the screen showed me, angling the screen Amelia's way so she could double-check. 'Imagined.Fluctuate. Problematic.'

'Imagined.Fluctuate.Problematic,' she repeated.

'That's the GPS-located square metre of the planet we're currently standing on.'

'It's actually a three-square-metre location, and technically we're on our hands and knees, but yes, I know.'

'Whatever. If we remember those three words and give them to the emergency services or whoever, they'll be able to come here and . . . investigate.'

'Imagined.Fluctuate.Problematic,' Amelia said again. 'Got it.'

This mini-achievement wasn't much to cheer about, but

it gave me an idea I couldn't believe I hadn't thought of before. Trying not to sound too hopeful, I asked Amelia how much battery life her own phone had.

'Not much. I took a fair bit of video with it yesterday.'

'Not much, but some?'

She looked. 'Sixteen per cent.'

I steeled myself to ask the question. 'And have you downloaded the What3Words app yourself?'

'After you mentioned it I did, yes, obviously.'

I puffed out my cheeks with relief. 'It has a navigation function. You don't even need data to use it. If Xander sends us his location, we can use the compass feature on the app to get back to him.'

I'd texted Xander and Amelia as I explained this, saying simply *Pls txt me + A yr W3W locn asap*. My phone took an age to send the message, but Amelia's pinged in response. Instantly the screen in my hand went black. No matter: if Amelia had received it, Xander would too, surely?

We knelt there, staring at her phone screen. It felt like nothing happened for aeons; in fact, Xander replied in just two minutes: *'Retrieving.Surer.Deafened.'*

Amelia's phone was already on low power mode. I watched as she shut down all the apps apart from What3Words. With *'Retrieving.Surer.Deafened.'* in the search bar, she hit the compass feature. Instantaneously it locked onto a destination a little over fourteen kilometres away, with the big red compass arrow pointing south-south-east across the frozen lake.

'Why did Kotler go this way?' I wondered aloud. 'If he'd carried on straight, he wouldn't have run across the thin ice.'

'Beats me,' Amelia whispered. 'Should we trust the phone and follow the compass, or retrace our steps, pick up our old tracks, and follow them?'

'Turn off the phone for now,' I said. 'But I reckon we should trust it. Fourteen kilometres won't take long on a snowmobile, especially over easy terrain. Kotler was taking the quick route home. This close to his own facility, he must have known the territory. But he turned off the direct route home and ran into this weak patch – it makes no sense at all.'

'Unless . . .' Amelia began.

I finished her thought for her. 'You think he could have fallen asleep at the wheel?'

'It's a stretch, but what other explanation is there? This open patch is pretty much the easiest to ride across, and a slug of weapons-grade vodka wouldn't exactly have helped him stay awake.'

We'd retreated – on all fours at first, then walking carefully – to our own snowmobiles as we talked. I slung my pack over my shoulder and climbed back into the saddle. 'I vote we head south-south-east at fourteen kilometres an hour – or as near as dammit – for sixty minutes, then we can use the compass on the app to zero in on Kotler's place.'

'Seconded,' said Amelia. 'You've got a sense of direction like a homing pigeon, so you lead and I'll follow.'

'And let's keep an eye out for odd-looking patches of snow as we cross the lake. I want to get off it in one piece.'

'Also seconded,' said Amelia.

Standing tall in the saddle to scan the snow as far ahead

as possible, I led the way across the frozen lake. Fourteen kilometres an hour felt so slow. I couldn't help thinking about what had apparently happened to Kotler. Could he really have fallen asleep driving a snowmobile? Despite my helmet, the wind on my neck was biting, even at that slow speed, and the engine noise was still a distraction. There was no way I could have drifted off while driving, but then again, the experience was new for me. Kotler drove snowmobiles all the time.

If we were right and he'd dozed off, veered towards the thin ice and crashed through the surface, the first he'd know about it would be the vicious slap of cold as he plunged into the icy water. It was dark. He'd have been disorientated, and he could have been dragged down by the snowmobile.

If he'd been pulled deep enough, he might even have bobbed under the ice, away from the hole. My experience in the avalanche had been hideous enough. If the snow had been freezing water . . . it didn't bear thinking about.

I tried to be methodical, scanning the snow ahead, looking for any discoloration at all, relieved to find none. Within ten minutes we'd made it safely to the reassuring undulations of solid ground. There were plenty of tracks through the bushes on this side of the lake. I picked up a route that headed in the right direction and tried to maintain a constant speed along it.

My eyes were still trained on the horizon, but after a time a quick movement made me glance to my left. An Arctic hare had stood up on its hind legs to survey us. It looked as if it was being pulled taut by an invisible string. As we passed, the string snapped and the hare morphed into a streak of white, disappearing across the snow.

The clock on the snowmobile's instrument cluster told me we'd been going for forty-five minutes. Shortly afterwards we came to a dense clutch of pine trees. The tracks I was following skirted them, so I did the same; though this meant leaving the south-south-east heading, the trees grew so close together that we had no choice. Just before the hour was up, I brought us to a halt and Amelia re-checked What3Words. While she was explaining that we were now within two kilometres of Kotler's place, but that it appeared to be back around the woods we'd skirted, a message landed from Xander.

*Get back quick. Caleb in bad way. Shockwave situation serious*, it said.

Since she still had more than ten per cent of battery life, I decided to keep the compass screen open and follow it, as fast as we could. In no time we were tracking round the far side of the woods. I sensed we were nearly there and the app agreed with me – or it could have been the other way around. We crested an incline. In front of us Kotler's facility was spread out, only a couple of hundred metres away.

I should have been elated to see it. But Kotler's apparent accident and Xander's text had filled me with dread and fear. We were arriving back all right, but 'back' was still the middle of nowhere, a long way from help for Caleb. And what exactly did 'Shockwave situation serious' mean?

# 36.

Xander must have heard the snowmobiles approaching. He was in the yard waiting for us. His hair was sticking out at odd angles: it looked like he'd literally been pulling it out with worry.

'Caleb's sick,' he said by way of a greeting. 'He's not right at all.'

'What sort of not right?' Amelia asked.

'He has a fever, and he spent half the night thrashing around in bed talking nonsense.'

'He's delirious, you mean?' said Amelia, dumping her bag on the floor.

'Something like that. At one point he tried to get dressed, saying he was going to walk home. When I stopped him, he took a swing at me then collapsed. And now he's out cold. I can't wake him up.'

We'd moved through into the bunk room, where Caleb was in bed. He was curled on his side, the hood of his sleeping bag pulled tight over his head. I knelt next to him. 'Caleb, it's me, Jack.'

He didn't say anything, but a shudder went through him. I put my hand on his shoulder and could feel him shivering.

'When did he last drink?' Amelia asked.

'I made him some tea yesterday afternoon, but he only drank half of it.'

'Has he taken anything to bring the fever down?'

'I looked everywhere for ibuprofen or paracetamol but couldn't find Kotler's medical kit.'

'I brought some,' Amelia said, and went to retrieve the pills.

'Here, help me sit him up,' I said to Xander. Between us we levered Caleb up against the pine headboard of his bunk. Despite the weight he'd lost since our trip to the Congo, he was surprisingly heavy. As we leaned him back against the bedframe his eyes flicked open. Hope surged through me, but his eyes immediately drifted shut again.

'Come on, Caleb,' I said. 'You'll feel better soon, I'm telling you.' I was trying to reassure myself as much as him. Amelia arrived back with a full water bottle and a pack of painkillers and we tried to get them into Caleb, but he wouldn't swallow the pills and most of the water leaked straight down his chest. That made his eyes flick open again, if only for a second, and he groaned weakly. These frugal signs of life were better than nothing.

'What do you think is wrong with him?' Xander asked.

I didn't think he expected an answer, but Amelia had one. 'I'm guessing it's Capnocytophaga.'

'What?'

'From the bite.'

'Capno-what, though?'

'It's rare, but Capnocytophaga is an infection caused by a dog – or cat – bite. Not everyone is susceptible, but if you are, and you're bitten, and the dog or cat – or wolf, I'm assuming – in question carries the bug, the symptoms can develop rapidly.' Matter-of-fact as ever, she went on, 'The bad news is, it can be fatal. The good news is, unlike rabies, it can be treated with antibiotics. We need to get him to a hospital – now.' As much to herself as to us, she muttered, 'It can't be rabies, anyway, because that takes weeks to develop.'

I was already plugging in my phone and scrolling through my contacts for Armfield's number. He picked up after one ring.

'Jack?'

As succinctly as possible, I filled him in.

'You say you have the W3W code for where you think Kotler went through the ice?'

I gave him the verbal coordinates.

'OK. You did well to mark the location. Leave that with me,' he said. 'Now, I'm currently on the *Polar Flow* in the Norwegian Sea. We're heading for port in Hammerfest, but it's five or six hours away. Tikaani's no closer to you by sled, and it will take Lukas at least four hours to reach you if he sets off now by road. Emergency services won't be any faster. But if you head cross-country on snowmobiles, you'll reach Route 92. It runs to the Norwegian border. Meet Lukas on that road, and you'll halve the time it will take you to get to me. There's a good hospital in Hammerfest.' He rattled off this plan with military precision. 'You're obviously familiar with W3W. I'll check the map, pick a sensible rendezvous point, and text you the words. OK?'

'Yes,' I said. 'But what about Caleb? He's too sick to drive a snowmobile, or ride on the back of one.'

'Kotler will have transportation sleds. Find one and hook it to the back of a snowmobile. Wrap Caleb up warm and make for the meeting point. It's not a long journey – take it slow and super-carefully.'

'Of course.'

'I'll hang up now and get Lukas on the case. Let me know when you receive my text. Keep trying to hydrate Caleb. We'll get him the help he needs, don't worry.'

'OK,' I said, and he ended the call.

It had taken Armfield less than five minutes to assess the situation, come up with a plan and explain it. Even though that plan meant we'd have to head straight back out into the snowy wilderness, I felt encouraged by his certainty. His sense of can-do was infectious. Yet, as I quickly told the others what he'd said, something niggled at me. I realised that, for all his practical, logistical help, Armfield hadn't shown any sympathy. Though I tried to ignore that, I couldn't shake it. A kind word wouldn't have cost him anything.

Xander had already packed up the bulk of his and Caleb's kit. Having ensured that all our phones were charging, he turned to complete the packing. Amelia sorted her stuff and gathered provisions for the trip. Meanwhile I set off to find one of the transportation sleds Armfield had mentioned.

I didn't have to search for long: three such sleds leaned upright against the wall in the nearest of Kotler's equipment sheds. The biggest was a couple of metres long and a metre wide, easily big enough for us to lie Caleb down in. But it had a lid, a bit like a roof box, making it look more like a coffin than a stretcher. We couldn't shut Caleb in it. I'd have to take the lid off somehow.

There was a workbench at the other end of the shed, with a tool rack above it. Kotler seemed to be the organised sort: all his tools were slotted between nails and he'd drawn felt-tip outlines around everything so he knew where to return them. Looking at the display and thinking of him drawing the outlines sent a shiver through me: I barely knew the guy, didn't much like him, but I hated the thought of him dead. I wanted to unscrew the hinges holding the lid to the roof box/sled, but on closer inspection they were riveted into the plastic, so in the end I had to use a hacksaw to cut the hinges free.

As I was dragging the stretcher sled out onto the forecourt, I caught sight of something orange tucked behind the door. It was the metal box I'd seen Kotler move out of sight the previous morning. Curious, I opened it. The box was empty. I nudged it with my toe. The thing moved easily enough. Whatever heavy stuff the box had contained when I'd seen Kotler shifting it had clearly been removed. The furtive look he'd given me came to mind. What had been in the box?

The sled had a fixed drawbar that slotted neatly into a receiving cup on the back of the snowmobile and locked in place with a sprung pin. The drawbar being solid meant the sled wouldn't run into the back of the snowmobile when it slowed down. Amelia, who had thought to refuel the two snowmobiles with petrol she'd found in the other barn, had also gathered some blankets from the house. We lined the sled with them, adding a pillow she'd brought from the bunk room to cushion Caleb's head.

Armfield's coordinates had come through: Publish. Unexplained.Birdman. I let Armfield know that we'd received them, and we turned to the task of getting Caleb into the sled. Him being cocooned in his sleeping bag helped a bit: between the three of us we carried him in it out to the waiting sled. Perhaps the cold air woke him: he started to wriggle as we laid him on the makeshift bed, then mumbled something that sounded like 'I don't want a bath anyway.' In the context this was pretty funny, and that, combined with my relief that he'd said anything at all, made me grin at Xander.

'You're all right, Caleb,' I said. 'Just a short ride, and we'll get you sorted.'

He tried to sit up, then rolled onto his side.

'Easy,' I said, turning him gently onto his back. 'Just lie still, rest up, and we'll be there in no time.'

Xander had unzipped an extra sleeping bag and tucked it around Caleb, who had stopped moving. Amelia said, 'Do you think we should strap him in somehow?'

'Seems harsh, tying him down,' I said. 'But maybe you're right. Better to be safe than sorry. I'll fetch some webbing from the shed.'

We wedged a couple of our bags on either side of Caleb's

legs. He didn't stir. The last thing I did, before shutting up the house, was to collect our phones and chargers. Lukas had messaged me: *En route to Publish.Unexplained.Birdman. ETA 16.45.*

That gave us just over an hour to make it there ourselves. I plugged the coordinates into the app and worked out that we'd need to sustain roughly nine kilometres an hour to be there on time, travelling as the crow flies. That would be easy enough over smooth terrain, but I had no idea what the ground we had to cover looked like. I tried to be positive: Armfield would have scoped our likely route and judged it navigable.

We got ready to set off. I was driving the snowmobile pulling Caleb's sled, and Xander would ride with Amelia. The mid-afternoon sky was white and cloudless and there was a stillness in the air which the snowmobiles tore up, roaring to life. We crawled south out of the yard. I led the way so that Amelia and Xander could keep an eye on Caleb, wrapped tight in the sled. I knew which bearing to take, but could only hope that a clear path lay ahead.

## 37.

The going was good at first. We cut across undulating hills iced in pillowy snow. It was tempting to open up the throttle but I held back, giving myself ample time to check and recheck the ground ahead of us. We couldn't afford an accident. Fifteen minutes in, we came upon a stand of scrubby trees, but they weren't densely packed. I threaded a way through them easily enough, staying more or less on course. We didn't run into trouble until we'd got past the trees. When we did, I was pleased I'd opted to go so slowly.

We were running up a gentle incline towards a ridge where the pale sky and slope of snow met. I brought the snowmobile to a halt before we reached it, and stood up in the saddle to take a better look.

The ridge was only a couple of metres high but it was sheer, with a bit of an overhang in places, making it way too steep for the snowmobile to run down. I looked left and right. The ridge stretched out as far as I could see in both directions. There was no way of knowing how far it extended; we'd have to investigate. Amelia had pulled up alongside me and cut her engine.

'Great,' she said.

'This wouldn't have shown up from above,' I said. 'If Armfield scoped out the terrain using satellite imagery online, he might not have seen it.'

'There'll be a way around,' said Xander.

'Which way should we look first?' I replied.

'Pointless question,' said Amelia bluntly. 'It's a fifty-fifty toss-up.'

'I vote north,' said Xander.

'Why?' she replied.

Xander shrugged. 'The more pointless the question, the better it is to answer it quickly and move on. We don't have time for a debate.'

With a glance back at Caleb, still swaddled in his makeshift stretcher, I did as Xander suggested and led the way north, tracking the ridge, hopeful that it would fall away or at least dip low enough for us to cross. But it didn't. Five minutes running along the top of the ridge turned into ten, fifteen, twenty. If anything, the sheer wall beneath the lip was bigger here than it had been where we stopped. Amelia pulled up next to me and we stopped again.

'We should try to the south,' she yelled over the idling engines.

I hate backtracking. Even if we shot back at twice the speed we'd come, we'd have wasted half an hour simply getting back to where we'd started. A gust of wind lifted a puff of powder from the ridge as we sat there dithering. I realised I was grinding my teeth.

'Hold on,' I said. 'We're missing a trick here.'

'What are you thinking?' Xander asked. Amelia crossed her arms, waiting for my answer.

Instead of explaining, I dismounted and unhitched Caleb's sled from the back of my snowmobile. Amazingly, he was awake, and even smiled weakly at me as I stood over him. I was elated. It seemed a good omen. If I had any doubts about my plan, they evaporated in that moment. I gave him a thumbs-up. 'I've got this, guys,' I said, and jumped back on the machine. 'Wait here.'

I steered away from the ridge and cut a wide arc across the snow plain. Turning back towards my friends, I set a course just to the left of them and increased my speed, gradually at first, but with fifty or so metres to go I let rip.

Jumping a mountain bike is all about committing. I guessed that jumping a snowmobile was the same. If you go slowly over a drop, you'll nosedive. From experience, I know that hurts. With a bike, you can make up for a slow approach by lifting the front wheel. But snowmobiles are too heavy for that. So: speed. I hit the ridge flat out, standing light on the skids and holding the handlebars loosely. Land rigid and with a death-grip on the bars and you're likely to bounce off a bike. Suck up the impact with bent joints and soft hands and you'll stay on. I was scared, of course I was, but just like with any sketchy sport, the fear is part of the fun. At the moment of lift-off, when the skids left the snow and the snowmobile shot into the air, I swear I was grinning.

And it worked! I knew the landing sloped downwards, and the snowmobile hit it at exactly the right angle. Unlike hard earth, the snow cushioned the impact. The skis sank deep. I still had the throttle open hard: the track bit and the snowmobile, having sloughed into the pillowed snowbank, surged out of it in a triumphant explosion of powder. I slowed down and cut a sharp turn back to the ridge. Amelia and Xander were standing above me. He looked comically impressed, but she had her hands on her hips.

'How do we get Caleb down?' she said.

'The sled's not that heavy. Between the three of us, we'll manage. Xander, jump down and stand on the snowmobile with me. We'll just about reach. And you guide the sled towards us, Amelia.'

Xander did better than a straight jump. He turned round on the ridge and backflipped the drop; a neat trick, though it sank him knee-deep. By the time he'd pulled himself free, Amelia had slid Caleb's sled to the edge. On tiptoe, standing on my snowmobile's saddle, Xander and I took hold of the skis. The weight bit into my gloves, bore down on my arms, spread heat into my chest, but the success of jumping the ridge made me strong, and I could tell the same was true for Xander: why else would he have pulled such a daft stunt? Between us we manhandled Caleb, in his sled, into the powder. His mouth was a compressed line of discomfort, but his eyes were still open. Catching sight of me, he forced a nod.

'Want me to climb up and jump your snowmobile down too?' I called up to Amelia.

'Yeah, right,' she said, and began throwing our bags down to me.

Once she'd dropped the lot to us, she retreated from sight. Her snowmobile's engine ripped into the silence, then faded, then roared again. It sounded as if she was heading straight towards us; I almost dived for cover under the ledge. But she flew off it well clear of us and made the jump look easy, landing in an explosion of white. She circled back to us and raised her goggles. Grinning, she said, 'I can't believe I didn't think of doing that myself.'

Xander was already coupling Caleb's sled to the back of my machine. 'We need to crack on, make up the lost time,' he said.

I rechecked the heading we needed to follow before we set off again, praying that we wouldn't hit another obstacle. And we didn't. In fact, before long we joined a straight track that took us in the direction of the road. A fence ran along the side of this track, though only the top third or so of the fence posts was visible, sticking out of the snow.

Had Armfield suggested this meeting point knowing that the track would make the last part of our journey easier? I suspected so.

The next time I paused to check my phone, we had less than a kilometre to go, and we made it to the rendezvous point a mere ten minutes late. Here, the road had been snowploughed. A drift stood in the desolate junction where we were supposed to meet Lukas. Had he parked behind the drift? I crawled the last few metres in the snowmobile, hoping against hope that he'd be there, but my heart sank as we rounded the final bend. His truck was nowhere to be seen.

## 38.

'He can't have come and gone already, can he?' Xander said.

'Of course not,' I replied, unconvinced. I'd dismounted from the snowmobile and knelt over Caleb. Steam rose in time with his slow breathing. His skin looked so pale against the darkness of his sleeping-bag hood.

'You're sure this is the right spot?' Amelia asked.

The question was irritating; I'd just looked. Still, it didn't hurt to check again, and in the nanosecond before the app opened, hope built that I had in fact made a mistake, since at least that would explain things. Perhaps Lukas was parked in the right spot – elsewhere. But no. I hadn't slipped up. We were where we should be, more or less on time, and Lukas wasn't.

'I could search up and down the road, see if he's nearby?' Amelia suggested.

This wasn't a bad idea, but instinctively I felt that we shouldn't split up.

'Let me call Armfield first, see if he knows what's

going on.' I looked to the western horizon of low-lying, tree-strewn hills as I waited for him to pick up. The sky was already edged in purple: we didn't have much daylight left. To be stranded on a frozen hard shoulder with no idea when Lukas might eventually arrive, was not an appealing prospect. No traffic passed. The wind had got up: the cold would cut us to bits before long. I realised I was expecting Armfield to answer his phone more or less immediately, because that's what he'd done every time I'd called him up to now, but the phone went straight to his answerphone message. 'To leave a message for Jonny Armfield, speak.'

I briefly explained our predicament and asked him to call me back as soon as he could. I was kicking myself for not having made sure I had Lukas's number. Why hadn't Armfield given it to us? Although I knew it was a long shot, I couldn't stop myself asking Amelia if she happened to have seen it written down, which was shorthand for asking if she'd mentally photographed it.

'If I had, I'd have said,' was her reply.

'Well, in that case I reckon you're right and we should have a quick scout up and down the road, just in case he's nearby but somehow in the wrong spot. Xander, you stay here with Caleb. Try to keep him warm and out of the wind as best you can. You look that way, Amelia' – I pointed down the road – 'and I'll head up there.' I nodded in the other direction. 'No more than five minutes out, five minutes back, OK?'

By way of answer Amelia pulled on her helmet again.

I quickly disconnected Caleb's sled from my snowmobile and we set off in unison, headed away from one another. The going wasn't particularly easy; I had to pick my way along the slushy hard shoulder of the road and every now and then it became a gritty tarmac. I dreaded to think of the state of the skids and belt, but what else could I do? I ran through alternative scenarios as I went: if Lukas failed to show up, we'd have to try to get back to Kotler's place. But how would we get up that ridge? We'd been able to jump down it, but we'd have to go round it on the way back. How far out of our way would that take us? Would we have enough fuel? If we got stranded overnight, we'd freeze to death. Sure, Kotler had taught us how to build an igloo, but we needed the tools to do it. Why hadn't we brought them? Even if we had, though, it was one thing to build an igloo in broad daylight, under instruction and taking our time, but quite another to do it in the dark. No, it would be better not to risk the return journey, but instead flag down a –

At precisely that moment, headlights appeared in the distance. As the vehicle drew closer, a weight lifted from my shoulders. I recognised Lukas's boxy black Mercedes 4×4. It slowed as it approached, and I realised there was something odd about the truck. Its headlights weren't symmetrical. There were three lights on the right and only one, a spotlight high up, on the left. Lukas came to a halt beside me. The two main headlights on the left had been smashed, and the bull-bar beneath them was bent in. What's more, there was blood on it. Lukas lowered his window and gave a one-word explanation. 'Reindeer.'

'You just hit one?'

'Hard. It came out of nowhere. I was going too fast.'

'Are you OK?'

'Me? Yes. But it isn't. Wasn't. I had to stop and put it out of its misery.'

'I see,' I said, wondering how he'd done it, and simultaneously not wanting to know.

'What are you doing here alone, anyway? Where are the others?'

This felt like a criticism, and an unfair one at that. I pulled my shoulders back. 'When you weren't at the meeting point, we split up to look for you.'

'Why would I be anywhere else apart from en route to it?'

'You could have got the location mixed up.'

'Wrong, you mean,' he replied, raising an eyebrow. 'I suppose it's a possibility.' He scanned his dashboard. 'As it is, I'm still 1.32 kilometres short of the rendezvous point, and so are you now. Dump that there. I'll come back for it later. Jump in.'

Lukas's clipped certainty came as a huge relief, but it also constituted a challenge: he somehow made me feel that the failed rendezvous was my fault, not his. Nevertheless, I did as he told me. On the short journey back to Xander and Caleb, I filled him in on our disastrous trek. He said very little in reply. I wondered for a moment whether this was because he felt responsible for what had happened: he'd picked Kotler, after all. But after a pause he said, 'Jonny explained to me,' and I realised that what I'd told him wasn't

187

news to him. Lukas went on. 'We'll have your injured friend in Hammerfest hospital in no time, don't worry.' Under his breath, he muttered, 'Provided I don't run into anything else on the way.'

## 39.

Amelia wasn't back yet, but Lukas ignored her absence and focused on Caleb. We pushed down a couple of seats in the back of the Mercedes so we could slide the stretcher straight into the warm truck. Caleb groaned as we picked him up but didn't acknowledge Lukas, even when he stuck an electronic thermometer in Caleb's ear and held his wrist to check his pulse. Having made his assessment, he pulled a sterile saline water pouch from a medical bag in the rear footwell, hung it above Caleb from one of the truck's passenger handles, rolled Caleb's hoody sleeve up above the elbow, calmly stuck a cannula into his forearm, and said, 'Rehydrating him can only help.'

As he finished this procedure Amelia's snowmobile came into view. By the time she'd dismounted, Lukas, having helped Xander and me chuck our bags in beside the stretcher, was already back behind the wheel, ready to go. Amelia must have spotted the damage as she got in beside Lukas up front. When he pulled away, gunning the big car forward, she said, 'More haste, less speed, perhaps?'

Thankfully Lukas appeared not to take offence, but he didn't slow down either. I checked my phone. A message had landed from Armfield. *Sit tight Lukas inbound*, was all it said. I texted back saying we'd met up and were en route to hospital. He must have hit a patch of proper signal as his one-word reply – *Good* – arrived instantly. To be in touch with him again felt immediately reassuring, and the fact that we were headed his way magnified the feeling. But again, his troubling lack of sympathy made it hard for me to relax, even in the warm, comfortable car.

'The journey will take a few hours,' said Lukas. 'You may as well get some rest. You must all be exhausted.'

He was fiddling with the car's touchscreen as he said this, and it turned out he was choosing some music to play. It was the sort of mellow acoustic stuff Mum likes, and it made me think of her. We'd managed to take some pretty spectacular footage of the sledding, the snowmobiling, the ice fishing and the threatened tundra landscape for our On the Brink entry. If all was well with Caleb, we'd hopefully get some more good stuff aboard the *Polar Flow*. I wanted to step up for Mum with the film. But I also wanted to get to the bottom of what Armfield was doing for GreenSword Investments. Xander was beside me in the rear of the truck. Quietly I said, 'The shockwave situation you mentioned: what does "serious" mean?'

He slid his laptop from his backpack and opened it, angled my way, then clicked through a bunch of screenshots he'd taken from the recesses of the dark web. Under his breath, he talked me through them. 'I managed to dig a bit deeper into the Valkoinen Karhu Energia Consortium that Finn Macmillan, via GreenSword, is so keen to invest in. There's a load of Russian names connected to it, and the few leads I've got on them point mostly to subsidiaries of Gazprom. That's the Russian oil and gas giant. Sure, they could be diversifying, looking to develop sustainable power initiatives, but they're still also pretty keen to rip the Arctic up in search of, well, more oil and gas.'

'Yeah, but where does the shockwave stuff come in?'

'Remember I found references to a disruption event? That seems to be what "shockwave" refers to. At first, like Amelia said, I thought it might be some sort of corporate code word for launching a hostile takeover of a power company, or perhaps a demonstration involving a bit of public disorder, but look at this.'

He clicked through to a blueprint for something that, if I'm honest, I couldn't have deciphered in a million years. The best I could do was see what it *wasn't*: a car, a computer, a clock, for example.

'Er, what's that?'

'I couldn't tell you from looking at it either,' he said, 'but it's linked to the disruption event. Here' – he clicked through to another image – 'this one was simply text in a language that I didn't recognise. They go on about this thing, whatever it is, in the context of DEW and EMP.'

'Come again?'

'They're acronyms, I think. DEW stands for directed-energy weapon, and an EMP is an electromagnetic pulse.'

'Hold on,' I whispered. 'You think this thing is a *weapon*?'

'A prototype for a new one, possibly,' he said.

'But what would they want a weapon for? Even if the consortium was as interested in fossil fuel projects as it is in renewables, that involves building stuff, not destroying it,' I said. 'Whose blueprint is this, anyway?'

'I've no idea where it originated. But some of these "investors" have shared the file, and the electronic paper trail leads from this thing, whatever it is, to the "shockwave" or disruption event.'

My mind was racing as fast as Lukas was driving. Ahead, the road was unevenly lit by our wonky headlights. Everything beyond the beams – and Xander's screenshots – was in darkness. How much did slippery Macmillan – and indeed Armfield himself – know about the consortium's wider activities? Though Xander is next-level with tech, it seemed impossible to me that he could have found out more than they knew. Did that mean they were in on whatever this 'shockwave' weapon was designed to do?

'One other thing,' Xander said softly. 'The same date and time are mentioned in these two messages. Could be nothing, or it could point to when the shockwave will happen. Look.'

He hovered the cursor over the date: *midnight on 8 April*.

'Do they mention where it's supposed to happen?' I asked hopefully.

'No.'

We had a possible date but no location, and I had no

real clue what a directed-energy weapon or electromagnetic pulse could do. 'Tell me what you know about this DEW and EMP stuff,' I said under my breath, checking my phone. Midnight on 8 April was just seventy-eight hours away.

# 40.

Xander told me that an electromagnetic pulse is a bit like a lightning strike. That's a huge, natural phenomenon, obviously. The most severe human-made EMP generator is a nuclear bomb, which is a bit like a million lightning bolts rolled into one. But as well as building these deadly, indiscriminate bombs, Xander explained that since the Second World War, weapons manufacturers around the world have been covertly developing targeted weapons that deliver smaller electromagnetic surges, capable of damaging electronic equipment and so on.

Directed-energy weapons are a more recent development – still in their infancy, in fact. Xander made them sound a bit like lasers, capable of causing intense, precise damage to stuff. So far, they've mostly been used as a defence mechanism for targeting missiles and the like, but recently there had been rumours of new, more attack-orientated directed-energy weapons.

'Do you reckon the blueprint has something to do with one of those?' I asked.

'I'd be lying if I said I knew, but it would be an odd coincidence if DEWs and EMPs were mentioned for no reason.' He shrugged. 'We could show it to Armfield, see what he thinks.'

That made sense, particularly given the deadline of 8 April, yet something in me resisted the idea. 'Let's think about it,' I whispered.

Up front, a flamenco guitar performance was playing on the car stereo. The music reminded me of somewhere hot, and since it had started to snow – swirling flakes our headlights bored through, making our speed seem faster still – it felt totally out of place. But Lukas seemed to like it, tapping the steering wheel in time to the music as we ploughed on into the night. I checked on Caleb from time to time: he lay there beside me, out of it for most of the journey, but as we pulled into the town of Hammerfest, I could see in the light cast by its streetlights that he had woken up. The saline bag Lukas had hooked up to him was three-quarters empty; maybe it was doing Caleb some good.

Lukas speared straight through town to the hospital and slewed to a stop immediately in front of it. We wasted no time in lifting Caleb out of the truck and carrying him through the hospital's sliding doors. An orderly met us there with a trolley: it seemed that someone had warned them we were coming.

'You three wait here,' Lukas told us. 'I'll get him seen to.'

It crossed my mind to insist that one of us went with Caleb. He'd want to wake up and see a familiar face, surely? But he was instantly wheeled away into a consultation room. As its door opened and shut, I glimpsed the reassuring sight of a white-coated doctor. She was wearing a name badge. I wasn't close enough to read it but noticed one detail: her badge was shaped like a polar bear.

We had been waiting less than an hour when Armfield arrived: the *Polar Flow* had evidently made good time. He brought a blast of cold air in with him, marching straight past the triage desk to where we were waiting. I stood up and he clapped me on both shoulders, meeting my eye with what, unless I was mistaken, seemed to be warm relief in his. Taking in Amelia and Xander, he said, 'Well done for making it safely to Lukas. How's Caleb?'

'We don't know,' said Amelia, her voice brittle. Caleb mattered to her. 'He's in there,' she went on. 'Can you find out?'

Armfield spun on his heel. 'Of course,' he said, and with the air of somebody used to going unchecked wherever he pleased, he headed for the door through which Caleb had disappeared.

If Lukas conjured a sense of capability, Armfield radiated it. Though it's daft, I even felt like Caleb's chances of a swift recovery were better now that he was on the case.

Soon Armfield, and Lukas, returned. Armfield looked serious. Perhaps I showed my fear at this, because he instantly tried to put us at ease. 'You did well to get Caleb here when you did. Bacterial sepsis, they think, caused by the wolf bite. Untreated, he could have gone downhill very quickly indeed. But he's on intravenous antibiotics and they've started to hydrate him. Rest and the treatment should knock the infection on the head soon enough.'

'Is he awake?' I asked.

'More or less.'

Amelia said exactly what I was thinking. 'Can we see him?'

'In the morning would be best. Lukas has sorted rooms for you in a nearby hotel. It's late now. Let's get you there so you can have a well-earned rest.'

'But what about you?' I blurted, hating myself for sounding so desperate. 'You're not leaving already, without us, are you?'

Armfield turned to me, an amused glint in his eye. 'Oh no,' he said. 'We're here overnight too. I'm afraid that Caleb won't be well enough to come with us on the ship, but Lukas has offered to stay here in loco parentis while we set sail. If you guys still want to come, that is?'

Relief swept through me, but it came out as, 'Let's see in the morning, shall we?'

'Right you are,' he said. 'Follow me. The hotel's just a short walk away.'

# 41.

We all had our own rooms in the hotel, and they were quite
a contrast to the igloo where Amelia and I had spent the
previous night. I was so relieved that it looked like Caleb
would be OK that I'd have crashed anywhere, but a double
bed in a warm room didn't hurt. I crashed out straight away
and woke with a start, having slept past nine. Immediately
I jumped out of bed, showered and got dressed, irrationally
worried that Armfield might sail without us if we failed to
show up early enough.

Amelia was already up and in the breakfast room
downstairs, tucking into a plate of steaming scrambled
eggs. 'Did you know that this is the northernmost town on
Earth?' she asked as I sat down.

'Er, no.'

'Except it's not.'

'What?'

'There are places further north, but they're not as big
as Hammerfest. Longyearbyen, on Svalbard, is the most

northerly permanent settlement, but the good people of Hammerfest call it a village and get to keep their title.'

'Fair enough.'

'Hammerfest also has a polar bear on its heraldic crest, but there haven't been any seen here for ages. The archipelago of Svalbard, on the other hand, is full of them.'

'How do you know this stuff?' I asked. 'We've been here less than twelve hours.'

'How do you think?' she replied, tapping her phone. 'You don't need a guided tour to find stuff out these days.'

'Fair enough. Anything else?'

'Er, yeah. Following on from what Xander told you about Valkoinen Karhu Energia Consortium's oil and gas interests, I found that that stuff – especially liquid natural gas – is pretty central to Hammerfest's economy these days. The town lives and breathes it. They're developing a massive new site to process more of the stuff pulled from wells beneath the Barents Sea.'

'Could be an unfair coincidence,' I said.

'Whatever it is, it's kind of ironic, given that Hammerfest was the very first town in Europe to install electric streetlamps, when everyone else was still using gas or oil to light their towns at night. Very long, dark winters this far north, I suppose: necessity is the mother of invention and all that.'

I helped myself to a mountainous cooked breakfast from the buffet: we'd barely had anything to eat in twenty-four hours and I was ravenous. Xander appeared, bleary-eyed, and did the same. We were just finishing up when Armfield and Lukas came into the breakfast room from the hotel lobby, their pace brisk as usual.

'I've come from the hospital. Caleb's condition has improved overnight. He's awake and making sense, but he's still very weak. They'll need to keep him in a while to be sure he snuffs out the infection entirely and regains his strength. The research voyage we're embarking upon is scheduled to last three days. It's up to you if you want to come with us – the offer is still on the table – or wait here with Caleb.'

'Let's ask him what he wants,' Xander said between mouthfuls.

'OK. In that case, we'll pay him a visit straight away.'

Xander was being diplomatic. He knew as well as I did that Caleb would definitely not want to stand between us and whatever we might discover – film or otherwise – on the *Polar Flow*. If he was in his right mind, that is. We headed over to the hospital to find out, Amelia leading the way. My cousin was sitting up in bed. He still had a drip in his arm and his face was as pale as the bedsheets, but his eyes were focused and he smiled at each of us in turn. 'I can't thank you guys enough for getting me here.'

'No big deal,' I said.

'Actually –' Amelia began, then cleared her throat and changed tack. 'Lukas drove us most of the way.'

'How are you feeling?' asked Xander.

'Not too bad,' Caleb said, his voice papery. 'Weak. Spaced.'

'They've got you on quite a cocktail of drugs,' Lukas explained. 'But the prognosis is good now, eh?'

200

Needless to say, I had been right: the hell we'd been through in the Congo had turned Caleb's former cockiness into selfless grit, and he wouldn't hear of any of us missing out on our voyage towards the ice cap. We'd be returning to Hammerfest in a few days anyway. He insisted that we go, and he'd use the time to recuperate. Provided he was well enough then, we could all return home together. Lukas confirmed that he'd stay in town until we made it back to port, and would check in on Caleb.

'I've done enough icy boat trips for one lifetime,' Lukas said wryly. 'Dry land's preferable, believe me.'

Armfield had been looking at something on his phone. Now he put it away. 'Right, we should board,' he said briskly. We made short work of our goodbyes to Caleb and hurried out of the hospital into the town, heading for the quay. It wasn't far – just a couple of streets away. I took in the town around us as we made our way there. Many of the houses were painted – shades of red, grey and yellow – and they all had white, snow-dusted roofs. There was a delay before we could board the *Polar Flow*. While we were waiting on the dockside Xander launched the drone to film the frost-bitten port encircled by the town, itself cradled by a ring of hills. On the monitor the land was a bleached grey-white, the sea black. He sent the drone up high and Amelia pointed out an island just offshore, full of pipes and chimneys and industrial clobber.

'That'll be the liquid natural gas facility I was on about,' she said.

I turned to look at the island. A twist of blue flame flickered above it, pulsing out of a tall, thin chimney. Seemed that Amelia was right about burning gas. Nearer by, I noticed that the dock walls were hung with tractor tyres to protect boats from the concrete walls. The lower rims of these tyres were fringed with snow: they looked like open mouths with bright white bottom teeth.

Interesting as that was, I was distracted by a woman wrapped in a huge orange parka who had arrived on the dockside near us. She was carrying a big blue bucket, from which she took a fish and dropped it into the sea. What was she feeding? I moved closer to look, expecting to see a seal or something bobbing in the water below her, but instead made out a white shape that brightened as it drifted up through the blackness to take the fish. It looked like some sort of dolphin, about four metres long, snub-nosed and milk white.

Amelia later informed us that the pale dolphin was a Beluga whale. I didn't know white whales were even a thing, never mind what they were called. It was an extraordinary creature, translucent and slow-moving, a super-solid sea ghost. We watched, transfixed, as the woman calmly fed it and talked to it and even leaned down to scratch its nose. When the bucket was empty, she stood up and walked back into town. Clearly this was a routine occurrence for her.

The white whale hung in the inky water for a moment or two after the woman left, hoping for another course, possibly. When one didn't materialise, it rolled away into the depths. I don't know why, but a shiver ran through me as it disappeared. Was Caleb genuinely OK with us leaving him? Would he definitely continue to recover? As Armfield shepherded us along the quay towards the boat, I wondered whether Mum would agree with our decision to undertake this voyage, given the circumstances, or whether she'd instead have wanted us to wait in Hammerfest with Caleb.

# 42.

I say 'boat', but the *Polar Flow* was really more of a small ship. Gunmetal grey, at some seventy metres long it was the bulkiest presence in the harbour by far. A stubby crane – with which the crew lowered and retrieved the submersible that was slotted amidships, among other things, Armfield explained – rose from its stern. Two sleek tenders were slung port and starboard for easy launch, either side of an open helideck.

The ship bristled with antennae and satellite dishes and strange white curved domes that reminded me of the Beluga whale's head. Its bridge had raked, slit-like windows facing in all directions, which made it seem as if the ship was squinting at 360 degrees of horizon at once from beneath lowered brows. Basically, it looked like it meant business.

On board, Armfield showed us to a cabin allocated to the three of us, which had two sets of bunk-beds bolted to windowless walls. There was a metal sink, a shower and a toilet in a connected, cupboard-sized room. The floor and walls throughout were lined with noise-dampening cork, softening the distant rumbling of the ship's engines, and the room smelled of diesel overlain by disinfectant.

We slung our kit on the spare bunk and followed Armfield up to the bridge, where he introduced us to Captain Lander, a tall woman who wore her red hair pulled back in a tight bun. She was tapping something into a touchscreen when we interrupted her, and barely paused to say hello.

Armfield explained that the captain presided over a skeleton crew of thirteen and that the boat was carrying fifteen researchers. There were workspaces on board, including a laboratory which, for this voyage, was stocked with imaging and echolocation kit. The purpose of this trip, he said, was to take a look at the seabed in a number of discrete locations. In search of what, he didn't say. He showed us other rooms on different decks: one was crammed with screens; one area was where the research team ate their meals (it smelled of curry); one equipment room was hung with scuba gear; and the storage area next to it housed an all-terrain vehicle. There was also a gym on board, with a couple of treadmills, a rowing machine and even some free weights, carefully strapped down in case of rough seas.

While Armfield was giving us this guided tour he explained that the *Polar Flow*'s Rolls-Royce engines gave it a top speed of 16.5 knots. What's more, the boat was rated as an Ice Class 1A Super, which meant it could operate in temperatures as low as −35°C, and its hull was reinforced to plough through ice some 50 centimetres thick at a speed of 4 knots. 'We won't need anything like that capability for this voyage,' he said. 'I'm just reassuring you that the boat is properly equipped to navigate the waters around here.'

'Where exactly are we going?' Amelia asked.

'I'll show you on the chart later,' Armfield replied readily. 'Basically, north into the Barents Sea to begin with, up round Bear Island. Then the itinerary has us doubling back to the coast. Finn Macmillan's research team have plotted it all out.'

'Is Macmillan on board?' I asked.

'He is. Timo from the consortium meeting is here too. Remember him?'

The cold, bald guy whose glasses had caught the light as he escorted us out of the lift came immediately to mind, as did the fact that our footage of the meeting had mysteriously disappeared. A shiver ran through me. I had an urge to ask if Armfield knew anything about the missing film, but somehow I couldn't. My excuse? I wanted the opportunity to see him at work first, with Macmillan and the others, to try to get a sense of where his true allegiance lay.

'Why don't you guys head up to the external observation deck? You'll get some good footage of the shoreline receding as we pull out of the harbour. I'll join you later,' he said with a smile. 'Right now I've work to do.'

The observation deck had been part of the tour: I liked how Armfield trusted us to find our way back to it. We arrived just in time to see the gangplank rise and the boat cast off from the quay. The rumbling of its engines dropped a notch and the black water to our stern boiled white. Armfield was right; the film we took of Hammerfest, swallowed up

206

by the expanse of rock and snow it sat within as we headed out to sea, emphasised the remote vastness of the landscape. A smattering of grey-black gulls rose from the dock and town behind it as we set off. They skimmed the boat's wake for a while before one by one they peeled away and turned back to shore.

Not long after the last of the birds left us, we were joined on the observation deck by Finn Macmillan. He glided out of the door, arrived at the rail beside me, and said 'Hey', as if we were old friends.

I nodded.

'Hear you had a bit of an eventful trek.'

'You could say that.'

'Wolves, and a dude through the ice, possibly.'

He seemed so flippant, I couldn't answer.

'Yeah,' he went on. 'Didn't think you kids were gonna make it back to us for a moment. Sketchy stuff!'

My grip tightened on the rail.

'But your buddy is on the mend, right?'

'We think so.'

'Well, that's something. And I bet you've got a load of killer footage. For the film thing. Which is a pretty good – a silver lining, I suppose.' The look in his eye as he said this told me exactly how seriously he wasn't taking our film, never mind Kotler's accident. He rubbed his beard and ran his hand through his tousled surfer hair. He looked more at home here, in a ski jacket, waterproof trousers and hiking trainers, than he had in the boardroom where we'd witnessed the boring – now deleted – meeting.

'Yeah,' he went on, 'and hopefully you'll get some stuff on the boat. We're heading up towards the ice sheet, so you may see some floes bobbing about. The money shot would be a polar bear sitting on one looking sad, I suppose.' He winked at me, making it clear that he was being ironic.

Amelia had drifted within earshot. 'What exploratory work is the voyage for, exactly?' she said.

'Checking out the ocean bed,' he said smoothly, 'in search of a good spot to tether a field of wind turbines.'

'Isn't it too deep for that?'

'Actually, the Barents Sea is pretty shallow in places. So apparently not. It's expensive to do well, but viable, given the new technology.' Vaguely, he added, 'We're looking into other stuff too, I'm told. The team's made up of all sorts of specialist nerds, oceanographers, et cetera. They'll be pretty busy but you may get to talk to them. Ask for yourselves. You know, really drill down, so to speak.' He gave Amelia's shoulder a gentle fist-bump, nodded at me, then headed back inside. There was something slippery about the guy. Or even worse. I trust my gut when it comes to people. Finn Macmillan had a catlike quality to him, both in his loose-limbed movements and in the way he seemed to be toying with us. The encounter left me feeling uneasy.

# 43.

On our first morning aboard the *Polar Flow* the sea was calm, a black mirror pulled tight to the horizon, its surface full of shifting, dark shapes. We took some footage from different vantage points around the boat, hanging over the prow to film the bow wave and dropping to the lowest rail behind the helideck to get some shots of the white foam churned up by the hidden, rumbling props. We also did our own backtracking version of the guided tour Armfield had given us, to get some film of different areas on board: our cabin, the gym and mess areas, even the bridge.

Captain Lander wasn't at the helm when we arrived there. First Officer Harvey, a wiry little guy with a neat black beard, gave us a warmer welcome than she had and said he was fine with us filming what was going on. The answer to that was not much. To compensate, he started talking us through the instrument cluster and boat controls: the depth sounder, the autopilot screen, the shortwave radio, panel of voltmeters and so on. Unfortunately, he was cut short by the captain's return. One look from her told him – and us – that we were an imposition she'd put up with for Armfield's sake. Without him there she didn't want us around either.

Despite the big breakfast I'd eaten that morning, the sea air meant that by midday I was ravenous again. We made our way back to the mess in search of something to eat, and found that the cook, a pale guy with a polished, shaven head and thick Scottish accent, had already begun to dish out the curry I'd smelled earlier. I ate two bowlfuls and Amelia had some too, but by now the swell had subtly built. Although it was still nowhere near rough, Xander didn't feel like eating. I remembered how ill he'd been during the storm off Zanzibar, but didn't mention it.

After eating, we headed back to our cabin. I suggested we ask Armfield for access to the ship's Wi-Fi network, but Xander didn't want to risk it. 'They can monitor what I do if we're working through them,' he explained. 'If I hotspot it, we have a better chance of staying under the radar.'

This made sense, as did his suggestion that he carry on trawling to find out what GreenSword was actually up to with the consortium while Amelia and I kept visible and filming. By now the subtle shifting of the boat in the water had built to a gentle roll, and I suspected that Xander preferred to cope with any motion sickness sitting down.

Back out on deck, a cutting wind had sprung up, serrating the burnished surface of the sea and generating a procession of shifting waves that lifted and dropped the boat unhurriedly. Whether it's the up-swoop of lift-off in an airplane, railing berms on a mountain bike, or the disorientation of being at the mercy of the waves at sea, I generally enjoy unexpected movement, and today was no exception: the alternating lightness and heaviness in my joints, stomach and ears put a smile on my face. But the wind was bitter. We filmed the distant sliver of coast, finding it impossible to keep still now, and nearer by, the shifting waves. Before long we were freezing so we went back inside and split up to explore the boat further.

I thought I'd pass the room Armfield had described as the laboratory and have a look inside if I could. No such luck; the door was shut. I stopped short of trying the handle and was glad I did because, as I stood there, I heard voices. I strained to hear what they were talking about, but couldn't make out clear words over the drone of the ship's engines.

Not wanting to be caught eavesdropping – especially as I couldn't actually hear anything interesting – I moved further forward and discovered that this wasn't in fact the ship's lowest deck: a set of metal steps at the blind end of the corridor dropped down to a small door. It too was shut, and locked, with a press-pad combination lock. Locked doors always make me curious to find out what's behind them. If I'd had to guess, I'd have said the bilge, since I was way below the water line already, but of course I couldn't know for sure.

As I was standing in front of this locked door, staring at the buttons on the combination lock, they lit up. Not individually, but all at once. I hadn't touched it! Was it some sort of motion sensor set to make it self-illuminate on being approached? What would the point of that be? Spooked,

I backed swiftly away from the door and took the stairs three at a time. I'd only made it a few metres down the cramped corridor before I heard a voice say 'Hey!' behind me.

Spinning around, I saw Finn Macmillan gliding up the stairs. He'd evidently let himself through the little door from the other side, hence its illuminated keys. He didn't sound angry at finding me there, more – as usual – amused.

'Lose something down here?' he went on.

'No, I . . .'

He waved away my explanation with a nod at my camera. 'Not the most photogenic bit of the boat, but each to his own.'

'What's in there?' I said, pointing behind him. If you want to know a thing, it's sometimes best to ask.

Looking unfazed by the question, he was nevertheless vague in answering it. 'Stuff. You know. Storage.'

I must have given him a look in return, because he stepped to one side. 'You want to take a look? Be my guest.'

The door at the foot of the stairs had swung shut behind him, so I couldn't see what was in there, and I assume it had autolocked. Macmillan didn't go to open it for me, but his offer seemed genuine enough.

'I'm all right,' I said. 'To be honest, I was just taking a walk inside to warm up. We were filming out on deck and it's next-level cold out there now.'

'Yeah, I poked my nose out too. I think we're in for a present from the north.' He grinned. 'Sea could get a bit lumpy. Still, I'm told this is exactly the boat to cope with a bit of weather. It's costing us enough.'

'For sure,' I said.

'Later, then,' he said, folding his arms.

I retreated along the corridor and past the laboratory, half-expecting to hear his footsteps following me, but before I climbed the stairs at the other end of the corridor, I looked over my shoulder. Macmillan was nowhere to be seen. Had he disappeared through the little locked door again? That made me pause: why had he emerged at all, only to go back in after I'd left?

## 44.

As Macmillan predicted, over the next twelve hours the weather and sea conditions deteriorated. The slow rolling of the boat got worse until we seemed to be wallowing and lurching and lunging in all directions at once. Xander chewed a fair few motion sickness tablets. They helped: he managed to carry on working on his laptop despite feeling rough, and he was tough about it, not once complaining. I knew better than to ask if he was making progress. He'd tell us if and when he did. When we checked on him, the screen lit up a face that was already tinged green and set in a frown of concentration. Amelia and I spent some time up on both the internal and external observation decks, watching the prow of the boat gouge holes and white spray from the oncoming black waves.

Armfield found us there and explained that they'd expected this weather. It might get worse before it improved, he said, but it wasn't set to last long. In the meantime, the boat was ploughing north towards its destination regardless. That's what it was built to do. He told us this en route to his cabin. Once there he opened his door to let himself in, and braced himself against the sill. 'When we reach the coordinates the team want to investigate,' he said, 'I'll see if I can get you a look at the tech stuff they do, the imaging and so on. Could be interesting for the film?'

'Sure,' I said.

'Will they be launching the submersible?' Amelia asked.

'Quite possibly. I'll let you know.'

As well as a neatly made bunk in the cabin behind Armfield, I noticed a table and chair bolted to the floor. The table had a deep rim around it to stop things sliding off it in heavy seas. I only noticed this because a folder lay against one edge of the rim, safely contained by it. Armfield invited us to join him in the mess half an hour later for dinner, entered his cabin and pulled the door shut behind him. Again, he seemed genuinely keen to help, and it struck me that all my suspicions, given how much he'd put himself out for me, looked pretty irrational.

This doubt in myself was short-lived. We got back to our cabin to find that Xander, whose face was still pinched with nausea, had news, and it had to do with Armfield.

'You know, when I first looked, I got so far, but I couldn't work out whether Armfield approached GreenSword or the other way around,' he said through gritted teeth. 'Well, now I have. Look.'

He had unearthed what had to be the first message in the chain of communication, and in it Armfield clearly introduced himself to Macmillan, offering his services. Furthermore,

Armfield said right from the get-go that he had valuable information about the proposed deal with the Valkoinen Karhu Energia Consortium. He talked about GreenSword having to 'finesse' what was on the table, and 'do what would be necessary to present the deal in the right light'.

Amelia read this aloud and snorted. 'That's got to mean orchestrate a cover-up, or something along those lines.'

'What's more, the investment they actually seem to be making, right now, is definitely to do with liquid natural gas and other fossil fuel infrastructure. There's a new Russian-backed pipeline that American investors – fronted by Finn Macmillan – want a slice of. The sustainability stuff looks, at best, like window-dressing.'

'And you're saying Armfield was involved from the start in setting up the deal?'

'It looks that way,' Xander replied. 'And I'll tell you what's strange. These messages were actually pretty easy to extract. Not originally; I couldn't find them when I first looked. But today I was just rechecking old leads and boom, there they were.'

Amelia, sitting cross-legged on her bunk, folded her arms. 'Did you turn up anything more on the shockwave disruption event?'

Xander shook his head with a grimace. 'Nothing. But don't worry, I'm not done yet.'

Hearing the news that Armfield was in on the true nature of the deal, had made the initial contact, and even seemed to have been involved in setting the thing up made me feel hollow. Though I was unaffected by the lurching of the boat, I felt a bit sick. I thought of Mum at home. Our On the Brink film entry was supposed to support her; in fact, it played into GreenSword's hands. Sponsoring the film – and our disastrous trek – was all part of their cover-up. Armfield was playing me – but for what? Money, I supposed. He was no doubt in for a huge payout when the deal went through.

I wasn't sure what, if anything, I could do to right the situation, but I wasn't about to give up. For now, it seemed best to play along with the guy, pretend we hadn't worked out what was going on. He'd packed us off out of the way for the first days of the trip: presumably that was when the real deal-making had been done. Now he had us captive on the boat, helping to document the cover-up. Xander gave me a ya-think? look when I asked if he was up to joining us for dinner. 'I can just about cope with nothing inside me,' he said. 'A bellyful of anything would be a disaster. Leave me to it here.'

The half hour had passed; if Amelia and I were to join Armfield, we had to get going. My balance is generally pretty good, but the boat was really slamming about in the waves and to reach the mess we had to hang on to the handrail as we made our way down the corridor. Ordinarily I'd have enjoyed the rollercoaster journey through the boat, but the prospect of playing dumb with Armfield snuffed out the fun factor. I felt grim.

# 45.

Armfield hadn't invited us to join him for dinner alone. Macmillan and Timo were already seated opposite him at the centre table in the mess. The latter stood politely as we arrived and said how sorry he was to hear of 'the incident with your guide, and your friend's illness'. But although these words came out of his mouth, he managed to say them in a way that made it clear he couldn't have cared less. His bald head shone beneath the strip light. I turned away to see Macmillan grinning. How could Armfield take these guys seriously – unless he stood to benefit from whatever they were up to?

The cook served us bowls of steaming hotpot infused with something that tasted like horseradish. The bowls would have slid all over the place if we'd let them, but following Armfield's lead I held mine with one hand and used the other to spoon the food into my mouth. Eating like that, with all the pitching and rolling of the boat going on around us, should have been funny, but it just made everyone silently concentrate on what they were doing. It wasn't until we'd finished and handed our utensils back that Macmillan offhandedly asked whether we'd got what we needed, film-wise. Not bothering to wait for an answer, he turned to Timo and started a conversation with him. The background noise of the boat made it hard to follow, but I heard the words 'yield', 'payoff' and 'cubic metres': business talk, not intended for us.

I felt Armfield's gaze on me, and turned to find he was indeed looking at me. Evidently my poker face wasn't working, because he asked, 'What's up?'

'Nothing,' I said.

'Swell getting to you?'

'No. Xander's looking forward to things calming down though.'

'You seem a bit weary, Jack.'

'When do we reach our destination?' I asked. 'You know, the shallow bit of seabed you guys are so keen to scope out?'

'First light tomorrow, more or less. Things should have calmed down by then.' Turning to Amelia he continued, 'Oh, and we are deploying the submersible. I'll get you a look at it, and you'll be able to film the crane in action.'

'Great,' I said, unable to hide my sarcasm.

Armfield's penetrating gaze narrowed on me. Macmillan was looking at me too, with that amused glint in his eye. I felt the urge to create a scene, yell at them both, let everyone know we'd worked out what was going on. I fought it back. Slowly, Armfield said, 'Maybe the sea's getting to you more than you realise, Jack. Why not turn in early, have

219

a good night's sleep, and perhaps you'll wake up feeling more enthusiastic?' Having made this suggestion, he calmly struck up a conversation with Timo about 'the latest news from our Slavic friends'.

If I'd been able to shove my seat back from the table, I'd have done so to make a point, but instead I had to clamber awkwardly out from the fixed table. 'You know what? That's a pretty good idea,' I muttered, as if implying that he didn't normally have them. Amelia had risen too, and followed me as I lurched out of the mess room.

I didn't head straight back to our cabin though, and Amelia didn't ask why. We sway-walked to the stairs and dropped a level to the deck Armfield's cabin was on. When we'd followed him there earlier in the day, he'd let himself in so swiftly, I doubted it had been locked. Amelia, intuiting exactly what I was up to, whispered, 'Give it a go. I'll keep watch.'

I had no idea how long Armfield would stay talking to his colleagues and didn't waste time pausing to think about it. I simply tried the door, which opened easily, and slipped inside.

The file was where I'd seen it last, neatly on the desk, up against its rim. I'd wondered whether this was the same folder that the consortium had handed over at the Helsinki meeting, but I doubted that now. That file had been bulky and plastic; this one was made of card and comparatively thin. I opened it and began flicking through the sheaf of papers it contained, not knowing what I was searching for – and, if I'm honest, not really taking much in. There were a few pages of handwritten notes, the odd spreadsheet, a drawing or two, but none of it made any immediate sense.

Quickly I stepped to the door and cracked it open. 'Swap places,' I hissed.

As Amelia passed me, I handed her the file and whispered, 'I'll keep him out of here if he comes back. See what you make of this.'

How I thought I'd distract Armfield if he returned, I didn't know. But as I swayed there outside his door, my heart loud in my ears and my palms sticky, I trusted myself to come up with something. As it was, I didn't have time to, and not because of Armfield. In under two minutes Amelia pulled the door open, calmly stepped over the sill and said, 'Let's get out of here. I'm done.'

'You can't be!'

'Well, I am.'

Even she couldn't have taken in all that information in such a short time. Granted, her memory is more or less photographic, and she reads twice as fast as anyone I know, but she does actually have to, well, read stuff for it to stick.

'We may not have another chance,' I said.

'To do what?'

'Read the thing properly.'

In response she dug her phone from her pocket and held it up briefly. 'Yeah, we will. I took photos of every page. And I recognised some of what was there. Let's head back to Xander and see if he can help make sense of it all.'

I hadn't thought to take pictures of the pages myself. That made me feel pretty stupid, but there was no point beating myself up about it. As we staggered back to our cabin, I contented myself with the fact that we'd got one over on Armfield. Given what we now knew about the man, getting back at him was – to me, at that moment – all that mattered.

## 46.

Amelia transferred the photos to Xander's laptop so that the three of us could look at them on a decent-sized screen. He immediately scrolled through to the diagrams. I'd sped past them, turning the pages of the file, but as soon as he brought the image up on his screen, I recognised what I was looking at: Armfield's file contained copies of the blueprint Xander had uncovered online, referred to in the context of directed-energy weapons and electromagnetic pulses. It wasn't the same drawing, but the resemblance, once Xander pulled the original up next to it, was unmistakable.

We pored over the other pages Amelia had photographed as well. The specifics didn't make a great deal of sense to me, but there were references to kilowatts and bore holes and carbon emissions and money, specifically dollars, embedded in equations, some of them two or three lines long. There were also maps, showing Murmansk and the north Russian coast, Bear Island and the Barents Sea, the Svalbard archipelago, the Arctic Circle, North Norway and Finland.

Somebody – Armfield, presumably – had annotated these maps with ruled pencil lines, each labelled with a number.

'Those don't make sense,' Xander said, pointing at the numbers. 'They're certainly not distances.'

'No, but they could be times,' I replied. 'Sailing hours, for example?'

Amelia pointed to Hammerfest and traced her finger along one of the lines leading out from it. 'We could be somewhere along this axis, for example.'

I pulled out my phone, opened Google Maps and waited for the blue dot showing us where we were to appear. When it did, I pinched the map down in scale until it more or less matched the one on Xander's screen and held it up for comparison. Though it was hard to say for sure, it did look as if we were in the vicinity of a point on Armfield's pencilled trajectory.

'Where does that end up, then?' asked Amelia.

'Nowhere,' I said, zooming in on the projected end of the line. 'It's just the sea, short of Bear Island.' I tapped the only land mass on the screen.

'Presumably it's where they're scoping out the seabed for the wind farm,' Amelia suggested.

Xander, meanwhile, was tapping at his keyboard.

'What are you thinking?' I asked.

'I was just wondering . . . no.' He didn't elaborate.

'Well, if we're about here,' said Amelia, pointing to where the dot placed us on Armfield's pencilled line, 'we still have this far to go, which tallies with what Armfield said about us arriving at first light.'

I couldn't argue with that.

Xander, scrolling through the photos again, paused to look at a page that, apart from some handwritten letters and numbers, was mostly empty. And what was there didn't make sense to me at first. I recognised the handwriting though: it was Armfield's, compact and assured, exactly the same as on the letter he'd written to me. One set of numbers slowly came into focus for me: *24000804*. Next to them were four letters: *SWDE*. I pointed to them without knowing why, then surprised myself by saying, 'Twenty-four hundred hours on the eighth of April, shockwave disruption event.'

Both Amelia and Xander looked at me.

'Plausible,' he said.

'More than that, credible,' Amelia countered. 'Too big a coincidence otherwise.'

My shoulders sagged. 'I can't believe it,' I heard myself say. 'He's in on that too?'

'Whatever "that" is,' said Amelia.

A heaviness spread through me. I felt utterly exhausted all of a sudden. I shut my eyes; nothingness was preferable to the implications on Xander's screen. Xander reads me well in general and somehow clocked how I was feeling.

'If we're roughly here on the line, and not due to reach the end of it until first thing in the morning, then we should probably turn in early so we can be up and ready before we arrive.'

'Makes sense,' said Amelia.

I didn't even have the energy to agree, but did as he said. I brushed my teeth, stripped to my underwear and climbed into my bunk in silence. Within minutes I'd blotted out the day entirely.

Sleep didn't bring relief though. I plunged straight into a nightmare. As ever, my dream was at once absurd and realistic, ridiculous and totally believable. I was underwater, in a sweltering jungle, running down our street. My ears were full of the sound of rumbling engines and screeching tyres and the whumping of an enraged gorilla beating its chest. Sharks were circling and a good friend was drifting out to sea. I couldn't find a lifebelt to throw out to him. Now I had a lifebelt, but he was too far away and my throw was falling short, again and again and again. He would drown soon. Meanwhile the useless lifebelt was on the pavement outside our house. And pirates were swarming onto the *Polar Flow*. They'd already tied us all up and thrown us in the hold. It was pitch black at first, but now I was blinded by sunlight that bounced off a rushing windscreen, a pair of glasses, a bald head. I was thirsty, famished, sick. There were flies everywhere. I was caught in a snare. The windscreen belonged to an open-topped Mini, which was swerving around a recycling truck and accelerating hard. Mum was holding our school bags as we raced down the street. It was happening again: I was ahead of my brother Mark, leading him straight into the path of the car. The gorilla noise was in fact a metal-on-metal smashing, astonishingly loud. And Mark was stretched out on the pavement in front of me, his bottom half pinned between the car and the wall. I knelt next to him on the seabed. The gorilla thundered through us and the shark closed in. Mum sat with her head in her hands for days, weeks, years. I bent over Mark. He was trying to tell me something. These were his last words, but I couldn't hear them, much less understand what he was trying to say.

I woke with a start, struggling to free myself from the bed sheets, and forced myself to breathe slowly until my heartbeat returned to its normal rhythm. Something had changed. It was the pitch of the *Polar Flow*'s engines. They were quieter now, more distant. And the motion of the boat had altered subtly too. It had slowed – or even, possibly, stopped. We were no longer plunging through high seas, but becalmed on a lesser swell. With no natural light in the cabin, I had to look at my phone to see the time. It was just after five. This far north, the sun would be up soon.

I woke Xander and Amelia. We threw on our clothes and headed for the observation deck.

# 47.

We'd only made it a few paces along the corridor when Armfield appeared at the end of it. He put his hands on his hips and did a passable impression of a smile. 'Great, you're up. I was just coming to wake you.'

'We were on it,' I said, needing to emphasise that fact. 'We're just heading for the observation deck.'

'I can get you closer to the action than that,' he said. 'Follow me.'

The others fell in behind him. Though a part of me wanted to resist, I followed too.

He took us to the stern and we emerged onto the low deck beneath the helipad, which housed the crane. The sky was clear: stars were still visible against the inky dark vault above us. They faded towards the east where the blackness was turning an extraordinary deep blue. The wind had dropped, and the sea with it. The water rolled, silver-black, towards a horizon empty in every direction.

A couple of guys in high-vis gear were at work on the

deck, inspecting a boxy-looking thing that had to be the submersible. It had been raised through a hatch to sit beneath the crane. Two cables connected it to the ship. One was coiled on the deck next to it; the other was attached to the stout crane-arm above it. Xander said what I was thinking: 'Wow, bit cramped in there.'

'It's not a manned vehicle, it's an ROV,' said Amelia, in a tone that suggested Xander had mistaken something obvious – a cat for a dog, say.

'Of course – an ROV,' he said cheerfully.

Amelia backtracked. 'A remotely operated vehicle. Basically, an underwater robot controlled from the ship and attached to it at all times. Unlike an AUV, or autonomous underwater vehicle, which operates remotely at a distance from the ship, like an underwater drone. ROVs and AUVs can be compared to pressurised, manned submersibles, which are basically mini-submarines. That thing there is bilaterally tethered to the ship and has no window to look out of: hence it's an ROV.'

'Hence indeed,' said Xander. 'Also, a person would have to be curled up in a ball to fit inside it. Just saying.'

The submersible was much smaller than I'd imagined: basically, it was a yellow and grey metal-framed crate bristling with lights, lenses, antennae, grab arms and other bits of unidentifiable kit. One of the technicians was busy double-checking it while the other rearranged the coil of cable and made sure the clasp above the submersible was securely connected to the crane. When the first technician gave the all-clear, the second operated the crane from a panel in the deck wall beneath it. First, he raised the submersible above the deck rail. Next, he swung it out over the stern. Last, he lowered it into the swell. I was pleased that Xander had thought to film this scene as it happened, but once the submersible was beneath the waves there was only the cable unspooling into the depths to watch, which wasn't exactly riveting.

'Want to see what it gets up to down there?' Armfield asked.

'Absolutely,' Amelia replied instantly.

'Come with me.' Briskly, he led us back through the ship to what he called 'the operations room'. We'd seen this on our guided tour: it was next to the laboratory and was basically a dark space filled with backlit keyboards and screens. Macmillan was in here, leaning against a wall, his arms crossed. He yawned when he saw us. 'Morning, kids.'

I bristled at this and said nothing back. Armfield noticed. He did his eye-narrowing thing again. But he didn't say anything – either to me or Macmillan – just steered us past him to a guy seated at one of the monitors, who he introduce as 'Popov the pilot'. This sounded like something you'd hear in a book for young kids, but he was serious: the man's name was Popov and he was the ROV's pilot. Controlling it was referred to as 'flying' it, and it seemed to be a skilled job requiring weapons-grade concentration. Popov didn't look up from what he was doing the entire time we were there.

Armfield, who seemed pretty knowledgeable, explained the basics. At 90 metres this was a relatively shallow flight for the ROV – it could operate at twenty times that depth. The pilot's task was to avoid the boat first and the seabed second, while guiding the ROV around its planned route. Although the submersible had lights to illuminate its surroundings, it was still pretty murky down there and how the guy knew where he was supposed to fly the thing remained a mystery to me. Armfield explained that, as well as taking film and still images of the seabed, the ROV was imaging it sonically. It would also retrieve a sample – of what, I've no idea – to be analysed in the *Polar Flow*'s laboratory.

The fact was, all of this seemed perfectly legitimate to me. Armfield was genuinely enthusiastic about what was going on, and keen to share it with us. If I hadn't known otherwise, I'd have said it looked like a research team inspecting the ocean bed for a site for a floating wind farm. And perhaps it was.

But there was something else much more sinister going on, and we only had thirty-eight hours to find out what it was and put a stop to it.

# 48.

We stayed in the operations room until the submersible began its ascent back up to the boat. Xander filmed Popov the pilot and the flickering pictures displayed on his screens, footage of footage in a way, and Amelia quizzed Armfield on what we were watching, but I zoned out a bit, convinced that the real story was happening elsewhere. Once the ROV had left the seabed, I told the others I wanted to watch them hoist it back on board and said I'd meet them in the mess for breakfast afterwards. When Amelia made a move to follow me, Xander put a hand on her arm. He understood I was asking for a moment alone.

I did go and watch the crew haul the submersible up out of the shifting sea. Water poured from it, silvery yellow: the sun was by now properly above the horizon. The guy who'd operated the crane before unspooled enough cable to set the machine gently down again. Once it was safely planted on the deck, he created some slack, making it easier to unhitch the clasp and stow the submersible below decks.

Macmillan watched all this too, standing next to Timo at the rail above me. At least, he stood at the rail where he could see what was going on; he and Timo actually appeared more interested in their own conversation. They seemed to be disagreeing about something. Timo's palms were upturned and Macmillan was shaking his head, looking disappointed.

I headed up the narrow flight of stairs to their deck, but didn't emerge onto it in full view. Instead, I paused on the upper step, my head below the bulwark. I was closer to the pair here, but not close enough to hear what they were saying. If they had come my way, I'd have walked straight past them, minding my own business, but eventually they headed off in the other direction, towards the steps that mirrored mine on the other side of the deck.

Moving quickly, I followed. I saw them turn left at the bottom of the stairs and, having crept down after them, I tailed them through the boat. Instinct told me where they were headed: the little room in the bow, through the door with the combination lock. And sure enough, that's where they went, me following at a safe distance, ready to pretend I was there by complete coincidence if necessary.

When they entered the final corridor, I waited for twenty seconds before sticking my head round the corner, just in time to see the door close behind them. Immediately I padded the length of the corridor, right up to the door, and put my ear to it, hoping to make out what they were saying on the other side.

The ever-present throbbing of the Rolls-Royce engines ran through the boat, but since the engine room was to the

233

stern and I was low in the bow, it was a gentle noise here. Nevertheless, it blotted out much of what I would otherwise have been able to overhear. I could only piece together occasional words and phrases that were loud enough to poke through the background rumbling. Timo's voice, harsher than Macmillan's Californian drawl, was the more audible. The first thing I heard him say was 'right under his nose'.

I couldn't catch Macmillan's response.

'And if they do salvage the wreckage, he'll be in it to take the blame,' Timo said next.

The first bit of Macmillan's reply was inaudible, but it ended with 'just not cottoned on'.

The two exchanged further words, but a jangling noise overhead – somebody moving something on an upper deck – muffled whatever it was.

I heard Macmillan's voice next. 'The timing's still super-critical.'

Timo's reply ended with, 'And don't worry, the copter pilot knows to get us out of here pronto.'

Macmillan said something about 'not underestimating' in response. Then he laughed. 'Everyone's a winner.'

'The weather is still a factor,' Timo said.

Macmillan: 'No worries there, set fair.'

Timo's reply was a mumble ending with the words 'collateral damage'.

'Publicity' was all I caught from Macmillan.

Timo, crisply: 'The share spike after we do the deal will be magnificent!'

Macmillan: 'Yeah, you're welcome.'

Timo chuckled and said, 'Give me a hand here.'

Then I heard nothing for long seconds.

'That'll do,' was the next thing Macmillan said.

'Yes, that will hold,' Timo replied.

'Kinda ironic,' said Macmillan. With my eyes shut, I could see him smirking. 'When you think about it.'

'As long as it works,' said Timo.

'It'll work,' said Macmillan, more assertively. 'Don't you worry about that.'

There was something conclusive about his words. I took a step back. Did I hear footsteps on the other side of the door, or was that my imagination? It didn't matter. I spun around and jogged to the stairs at the end of the corridor. If they'd opened the door and seen me hotfooting away, that would have been bad, but I counted on getting out of sight before they emerged. It turned out, I made the right choice.

## 49.

I kept on back to our cabin, running through the snippets of conversation I'd overheard to cement them in my mind. Amelia and Xander were already there.

'Where'd you get to?' Amelia asked.

I explained.

'And what did you hear again, precisely?' she asked, pulling out her phone.

As I recounted what Macmillan and Timo had said, she keyed in the phrases one-handed, looking as much at me as at the screen. When I finished with 'Don't you worry about that' she inspected her transcript, a look of intense concentration – which in her case includes the hint of a smile – on her face. Gaps and all, the transcript was a code she could now puzzle over.

'Sounds like they have some sort of plan to rig the deal,' Xander said.

'What do you mean?'

'The bit about the share spike. I'll bet the whole shockwave disruption event thing is designed to shift the share value.'

I'm no expert on stocks and shares, and I must have looked a bit blank. Xander went on. 'If they do something to bring a share's value down or pump it up just before or after they buy or sell, they can make a load of extra cash on the deal.'

This made sense, but weirdly it also made the shockwave event seem less interesting. If it was just about tweaking the value of shares in a company, so what?

'I concur, Xander,' said Amelia, still intent on her phone. 'But from what you overheard, I'd say there's a fair amount of uncertainty in play. In just under one hundred and ten words I count twelve, possibly thirteen, instances of doubt or hubris.'

'Hubris?'

'Originally, defiance of the gods. Now, ignoring a likely outcome by sticking one's head in the sand, plus protesting too much. I mean, they sound like they're trying to convince themselves their plan will work without necessarily believing it. Phrases like "No worries there", "Yes, that will hold", "Don't you worry about that" and "Everyone's a winner". Get it?'

'I see what you mean when you read those phrases back out of context,' I said. 'But trust me, the whole conversation sounded pretty confident to me.'

Amelia looked at me sceptically.

'I found one piece of online information to support my share price theory last night,' Xander said, tapping at his laptop. 'Look, this is in the public domain. It's an "in brief" piece from a site called Energy Central News, and it reports that a deal between GreenSword Investments and Valkoinen Karhu Energia Consortium, taking a stake in the Nordic next-generation power project, is – "with a favourable wind", how cheesy is that? – set to complete this week. Pretty vague, I know. But what stood out to me was the bit that says that the "portfolio investment" is made up mostly of "wind and nuclear infrastructure, but also potentially liquid natural gas".'

'I wonder how much is riding on that "potentially",' Amelia said.

'When was that piece published?' I asked.

Xander checked. 'Three days ago.'

'And what day is it today?' I asked.

'Thursday,' said Amelia. '7th April.'

'So, tomorrow is Friday.'

'That's the way it generally works,' said Xander.

'And Friday is generally the end of the working week,' I said.

'Not necessarily, with deals like this. But possibly,' said Xander.

'Where are we now?' I asked. 'In relation to the lines on Armfield's nautical chart?'

Amelia had her phone to hand. She cross-referenced the photos she'd taken of Armfield's annotated chart with the location beacon in Maps. 'Further north. Here-ish. Just past Bear Island.'

Looking at the dot of the island surrounded by sea, I had the sudden urge to clear my head in the fresh air. 'Either of you want to take a look on deck with me?' I asked, pulling on a fleece, my snow coat, a hat and mittens. Both did, and made similar preparations against the cold.

Since raising the submersible the *Polar Flow* had tracked northward, and the sea through which it was moving had changed: the great grey undulating slab of coldness was now pricked with gobbets of ice. Not icebergs, as such; these were smaller chunks that had broken from the sea ice and drifted south. They gave way easily enough before the boat's blunt prow, brushed aside with the bow as the *Polar Flow* nosed forward.

'The sea ice rarely makes it south of here these days,' Amelia informed us. 'If it does, about now, April, the end of winter, is the likeliest time for it to happen. And chunks of ice can still, statistically speaking at least, head right down into the oil fields. Rigs to the south look out for rogue icebergs and they're built so that they can be untethered and towed out of the way to avoid a collision. See how this stuff is moving with the swell though? It's drift ice, floating on top of the water, and it presents no problem. Real icebergs sit low and heavy in the water: the vast bulk of their mass is below the surface.'

Far off to our south-west a slab of land rose abruptly from the ice-strewn sea. Treeless, snow-scraped and sheer-sided, it was a pretty inhospitable-looking place, yet I was still pleased to be within sight of land again.

Spray rose from the foot of the cliffs: though the sea was calm offshore, waves battered the shore. With the land to give the sea a sense of scale, it was mesmerising to stand on the forward observation deck and watch the *Polar Flow* muscle on through the increasingly icy sea. Within half an hour we'd made our way into a bigger expanse of drift ice. Here the boat had to cut a path through a more or less unbroken sheet of the stuff. It wasn't thick, and the boat didn't even appear to slow down, making our progress all the more amazing to watch. Cracks shot out from the ice sheet, chunks broke off it, and we cut through the black water beneath it as easily as a bike tyre crunches through thinly crusted snow.

When I pointed this out, Amelia said, 'Yeah, this is the marginal ice zone. Get into the heavier pack ice further north and it wouldn't be the same.'

The three of us stood in silence for a while. Dots – birds – rose from the cliffs of distant Bear Island. They swept across the face of the rock and disappeared. Meanwhile, the *Polar Flow* rumbled on.

I became aware of a presence behind us. I knew who it was before I turned around: Macmillan. He smiled at me. 'Epic view, eh?' he drawled.

There being no alternative, I nodded.

'Kind of humbling,' he went on. 'Puts everything in perspective.'

'What do you mean, "everything"?' asked Amelia. The question was genuine, but it came out a little sarcastic.

Macmillan, marvelling at her, said, 'Huh.'

Xander said, 'I agree, it's epic.'

'Well, enjoy it while it lasts,' said Macmillan, making the view instantly less enjoyable for me. Did he mean we should enjoy the landscape while we were here, in it, or was he referring to the fact that the sea ice around us was under threat, all the way to the Pole? His glib tone didn't help. It turned out he was referring to our route, as he went on to say, 'We'll be headed back south again soon.'

'Why did we come up here in the first place?' Amelia asked.

Macmillan put his fur-cuffed mittens on his hips and winked at her. 'Why do you think?'

'Research purposes, I assume,' she said. 'But specifically?'

Macmillan chuckled. 'Wrong answer. We're here for you.'

'How so?' asked Xander.

Shrugging, Macmillan said, 'I thought you'd need some footage of the actual sea ice. The stuff that's under threat. For the film?'

Xander had brought the drone up on deck with him, but none of us had thought to deploy it yet. I felt guilty at the oversight, or wrong-footed by it at least.

Macmillan bounced on the balls of his feet. 'I mean, obviously I'd rig up that sad polar bear I mentioned to complete the scene if I could, but there's a limit . . .'

My mittens balled into fists at my sides at this and I muttered, 'Shockwave' under my breath. I don't know why; it just slipped out.

Macmillan didn't hear. Or at least, he didn't appear to hear. But Xander, standing next to me, definitely did. 'No, we appreciate it,' he said quickly, brandishing the drone. 'I was just about to put this thing up. The light's great.'

'Now's the time,' Macmillan agreed, and took a step away. Something stopped him from leaving entirely though. He turned back to Xander. 'You must have a fair bit of footage by now. Where's it all stored?'

'On my laptop,' said Xander.

Macmillan winced. 'Oof,' he said. 'Bit sketchy to have all your eggs in one basket at this stage, don't you think?'

Was he goading us about the missing footage? I bit my tongue. Now wasn't the time to make the accusation.

He went on smoothly, 'Tell you what, once you've got what you need out here' – he waved at the horizon – 'edit down the highlights, just roughly . . .'

'We've already started doing that,' Amelia cut in. 'Obviously.'

'Great, great.' Macmillan took off one glove, rammed his hand inside his jacket, and magicked up a business card. 'Well, once you've added the latest stuff to it, mail a rough cut of everything so far to this address, all right?' He paused, then added, 'Would you be able to do that by lunchtime tomorrow, say?'

Although this was phrased as a question, it was clearly an order. But just in case we hadn't understood, he added, 'We're paying for it, after all, in a way.'

'Of course,' Xander said.

Macmillan had pulled on his mitten again. 'Great, great,' he said again, and offered up his fist for Xander to bump his against. Compared to Xander's, Macmillan's mitten was enormous, a cushioned mass as big as a boxing glove. 'Good luck with it,' he said softly, with the air of a man who'd got what he'd come for. 'Good luck with it.'

# 50.

We launched the drone, flew it high up above the *Polar Flow*, and filmed the ship's progress through the ice. Xander was right; the cloud had broken up and the sun was less diffuse, more directional, spearing the incredible landscape with shafts of white light. As he dropped the drone closer to the boat, its shadow was clearly visible moving across the shattered ice in our wake. We'd rounded the island and were heading south again now.

I took all this in but my mind was elsewhere, racing. Xander's online research, the contents of Armfield's folder, the snippets of conversation I'd overheard between Timo and Macmillan – they all suggested they were plotting something bad. The 'deal' with the consortium wasn't what it appeared. At the very least, it involved fossil fuels as well as renewables. But they were also rigging it somehow. And we were being used to help cover up what was going on.

Armfield had seen an opportunity: fund a kids' eco-film and make GreenSword look good while they were doing the opposite. He'd organised an incredible trek – sure, it had gone wrong, but we still had some great footage – and neatly parked us out of the way while we were on it. Next, he'd brought us in close, close enough to keep tabs on us while Macmillan and Timo closed the actual deal. I felt used, manipulated, betrayed. And I had to do something about it.

But what?

At the very least, we had to raise the alarm. The trouble was, our information was so incomplete. A few blueprints of something that could be an electromagnetic pulse device or a directed-energy weapon, plus vague details of a deal already in the public domain. We didn't have a 'target'. All our footage – of the threatened landscape and the work research vessels like the *Polar Flow* were doing to scope out sites for wind farms – appeared totally legitimate. The only extra detail we knew, or we thought we knew, at least, was the suggested deadline: midnight on Friday 8th April. A day and a half away.

That afternoon, cooped up in our cabin, we worked on two things together. The first was the rough cut of our film. Amelia had told Macmillan we'd already made a start. While that was true, we still had a huge amount to do. Editing film is time-consuming. Between us we'd taken a lot of footage. And so much of it was good. Choosing what not to include was tough. We sped up the footage to run through it more quickly, but if we viewed it at anything above quadruple speed we risked missing details, so the process still took ages. I kept reminding Xander and Amelia that we weren't trying to create a masterpiece at this stage;

it was a question of cutting out the dead wood so that we could save all the good stuff. And I wasn't about to rely on Macmillan for that. Although I knew it would take ages to upload and download such a big file, I wanted Xander to send it to me, Amelia and Mum via WeTransfer for safe-keeping.

While Xander spearheaded the work on the film, I pulled together what we had on 'shockwave' and our wider misgivings about GreenSword and Macmillan. Mum would know what to do with this information. I knew she'd take me seriously, and I knew she'd alert the relevant authorities if she thought it necessary. I also knew she'd trust me to do what I could to find out more in the hours we still had left, and take any steps I could to sort things out.

The difficulty I had, with Mum in particular, was Armfield. Somehow, I couldn't fully implicate him. It seemed too cruel to let on that I suspected he was in cahoots with Macmillan, was using me, and stood to benefit from whatever crooked deal GreenSword was pursuing. I toned down my concerns and wrote only that Armfield was too close to Macmillan for me to risk raising my suspicions with him at this stage. But I included copies of Armfield's photographed notes in the document; she could draw her own conclusions from them.

Though we worked all afternoon, we still hadn't finished by dinner-time. We arrived in the mess to find Armfield, Macmillan and Timo already at a table with, among others, Popov the pilot. This suited me – we got to sit on our own. I shovelled down a bowl of creamy chicken supreme quickly. We still had so much to do. Portholes ran down one side of the mess. They were full of reflected light: it was dark outside now. As we stood up to leave, Armfield broke from his conversation, looked my way, raised a thumb and nodded. His clear-eyed gaze seemed unconcerned, his greeting genuine. I didn't know what to make of it.

After dinner, it took me a while to finish my dossier for Mum. Amelia and Xander paused in their film-making to review it before I pressed send. Xander said, 'Looks good to me' but Amelia – as I knew she would – suggested some tweaks. 'Prioritise the blueprints,' she said. 'Insist she gets them to somebody who will know what that machine is. Also, you're too soft on Armfield: his notes make it clear that he's in the know. That should be a full stop and start a new paragraph here and –'

'I get it,' I said, struggling to mask my irritation. She was right about the punctuation and the importance of the blueprints, obviously. But about Armfield: what did she know? 'I'll make the changes,' I said. 'And once I've sent this, I can help you guys.'

Just before midnight, I sent what I had to Mum. To be sure she'd see it, I messaged as well, telling her to check her email. Amelia and Xander still hadn't finished the edit. We spooled through more footage into the small hours, but it soon became apparent that to finish properly we'd have to stay up all night, and something told me we'd need to be rested – and alert – in the morning, so I called a halt. Bleary-eyed from so much screen-squinting, we all went to bed.

Whereas the night before I'd been plagued by bad dreams,

that night my subconscious gave me a break. I'd become a sluggish device with too many apps open, all of them competing for my processing power. Sleep rebooted me. I awoke feeling ready for anything.

## 51.

Unfortunately, feeling ready for anything is no use if nothing's happening. It's just frustrating. And that's how the following morning began. I woke up at six and immediately scanned my messages for a reply from Mum, but there was none. We were two hours ahead of her in England. Perhaps she hadn't seen my message before she went to bed, and the time difference might explain a slow response in the morning. At seven-thirty her time I called, but she didn't pick up. Then at quarter to nine I finally received a text which simply said *Can't get through to you? Don't jump to conclusions or do anything rash. I'm looking into it.*

She clearly didn't realise the seriousness of the situation. I tried calling back to put her right but, just as she apparently hadn't been able to reach me, her phone now went straight to her voicemail. In exasperation I sent more texts, but they too went unanswered.

Meanwhile, Xander and Amelia ploughed on with the film

edit. It was turning out to be much more time-consuming than we had imagined. We hadn't even got to the footage of the submersible yet; that, together with the ice-breaking, would take a while to pare down. I was all for chopping together stuff more or less at random, just to get Macmillan off our backs, but Xander was adamant that we should do the job properly. Amelia agreed with him. 'The film could well be the only good thing that comes out of this trip,' she said.

I could see her point, but still. It occurred to me that if Macmillan simply wanted us out of the way, then hitting us with this draconian deadline was a good way of achieving that end. Although I kept the thought to myself, it made me antsier still. The morning ground on. We couldn't all work on the film together productively at the same time, so I went back to looking through the material I'd sent Mum, trying to see it through her eyes and wondering why she wasn't more alarmed by the implications of what we'd discovered. Was it all a bit vague, perhaps? Was the 'disruption event' some corporate tactic after all, and the blueprint of the machine somehow a joke? The more I looked at the notes, the screenshots and the conversation snippets, the more I began to doubt myself, until suddenly I couldn't bear being cooped up in the cabin a minute longer. I had to get out, immediately, and do something, even if I didn't know what.

'You guys OK to finish up?' I asked. 'The end's in sight now, right?'

'Sure,' said Xander without looking up from his screen.

'Cut that bit in next,' Amelia said to him, not me. Then,

'Yeah, whatever, we'll make the deadline, and we'll see you for lunch.'

I headed out on my own, unsure where I was going, just intent on taking another look around the *Polar Flow*. We were well clear of the ice now, headed south through water as black as ink. From the lower rear deck, I watched the white spume churned up by our propellers spread out and melt away to nothing. A couple of gulls circled the boat, high above us, cutting back and forth across our wake. I skirted the stubby crane, walked up the gangway to the helipad, crossed it and re-entered the boat amidships.

Technicians were at work in the laboratory, doing what, I had no idea. The operations room stood empty. The workspace next to it was full, however: through the open door I caught sight of Timo and Macmillan holding court. The latter, spotting me, gave me an ironic salute. It made me want to punch him, but what would be the point in that? I moved on, realising that the gesture was meant to make me do exactly that: it was at once mock-friendly and unwelcoming. Maybe that's why the salute – and everything about Macmillan – annoyed me so much: though he seemed so chilled and accommodating, he was in fact controlling, manipulative, fake.

I worked my way up to the bridge. Captain Lander and First Officer Harvey were there, bent over a screen, in the middle of a discussion. Neither noticed me stop in the doorway behind them.

'If he wants us in this close, so be it,' said Lander. 'It's no skin off my nose.'

She stood back from the screen and put her hands on her hips.

The first officer said, 'Yes, but why the late change? What's the point?'

'Who cares?' said Lander. 'It's hardly a difficult manoeuvre. They chartered the boat. They've got the relevant permissions. Our job is to navigate the prescribed route safely.'

Harvey, lips pursed, breathed out hard through his nostrils, shaking his head. 'If I knew the purpose of it, I'd be happier.'

Captain Lander shrugged. 'Don't overthink it.' She raised her hands to the back of her head and yanked her red hair more tightly through the elastic band that held her ponytail in place. Amelia does the same thing when she's drawing things to a conclusion. Turning, Lander caught sight of me. Unease flickered in my chest: she'd been dismissive of us before, so would she berate me for being there now? Far from it. She seemed to welcome the diversion. 'Hey,' she said with a smile. 'I saw you send that drone up. Are you pleased with the footage so far?'

'Definitely,' I said. I felt compelled to add, 'Thanks for having us on board' but kicked myself afterwards as it sounded so stilted.

She smiled. 'You're welcome,' she said, and turned back to First Officer Harvey.

From the bridge I made my way to the forward observation deck. The visibility was good, the sky above us clear, the curve of the sea uninterrupted to the horizon. I had nothing concrete to navigate by and it occurred to me – more as a feeling than a thought – that I only had one real option, and that was to confront Armfield. Although I didn't trust him, he was no Macmillan. We were connected. Even if I didn't like it, I had to admit that fact. I'd talk to him at lunch, tell him we knew something was amiss, and ask him for an explanation. He'd probably lie to me, but at least I'd give him the chance to come clean.

## 52.

By now I knew the cook would be serving lunch, so I threaded my way back through the ship to the mess, where I was greeted by the smell of coriander-topped fish chowder, a bowl of which I demolished on my own while I waited for the others to arrive, fetch their own helpings and join me. They'd sent the film minutes before, Xander said. He looked genuinely relieved, proud in fact, to have submitted the edited footage by Macmillan's deadline. I couldn't help feeling pleased for him.

'Great work, well done,' I said.

'Has to be said, it's a slick first edit,' said Amelia. 'But there's masses more still to be done at home.'

Macmillan, dressed in a Norwegian fisherman's jumper – thick knit, dark blue with flecks of white and a deep ribbed neck – padded into the mess a few minutes later, after Timo and a couple of technicians. Before collecting his own meal he swerved over to our table. 'Guys, I've not looked at it yet, but I saw the message and clocked the attachment. Well done getting the film in on time.'

Xander shrugged modestly.

Amelia said, 'Until you've watched it, you can't be sure it's a worthy effort.'

'I trust you,' he said, grinning at me. 'We're due back in port in the small hours. Enjoy the rest of the trip until then.'

Trusting him and enjoying our remaining time on board the *Polar Flow* were both impossible. Right now, I just wanted to speak to Armfield. But although we stayed at our table all the way through the lunch sitting, he didn't show up in the mess. Xander headed back to the cabin. Amelia stayed with me until everyone else had left, then said, 'Why are we waiting exactly?'

I explained what I'd decided to do.

She narrowed her eyes. 'In the absence of a further breakthrough, I suppose that's a sensible option.'

'If he doesn't show in the next few minutes, I'll go to his cabin,' I replied.

'Sure, do that,' she said. 'But don't expect him to give you any answers.'

I let ten minutes slide past. The cook began to wipe down all the floor-bolted furniture – tables and seats alike – with a bright blue dishcloth. When only our table remained for him to do, I stood up to go. Amelia fell in behind me, but I stopped her. 'It's probably best if I have this conversation alone.'

'Are you sure you have all the detail at your fingertips?' she couldn't help asking.

'Enough of it.'

'Suit yourself,' she said matter-of-factly. 'I'll go help Xander.'

With a heavy heart I trudged down a deck and forward to Armfield's cabin. Up until that moment, a part of me had still been hoping against hope: now I was resigned to the fact that this conversation could only bring bad news. I almost turned back. But I had a duty – to Mum, and to myself – to confront Armfield and get to the bottom of what was going on.

Steeling myself, I knocked on his door.

There was no answer.

I knocked again.

Nothing.

Again, harder.

Not even a rustle. He wasn't in there. The anti-climax tasted like a mouthful of dirt: I've eaten enough of it falling off my mountain bike over the years. Still, I had to climb back into the saddle. If he hadn't been at lunch, and he wasn't in his cabin, he had to be somewhere else on the ship. I did another lap, from the bridge to the bilge and from the stern to the bow, but I didn't run into him. There were plenty of closed doors I couldn't see through, however: he had to be behind one of those, I assumed, in a meeting with GreenSword's technicians or Timo's men or the ship's crew. It was beyond frustrating – infuriating, in fact – not to be able to have it out with him now that I'd decided to do so, but I wasn't about to change my mind. I'd give it an hour then look for him again.

In the meantime, I sent him a text. *Need to talk to you* is all it said.

I'd half expected an immediate reply, but none came, so I retreated to our cabin to wait. On the way, it occurred to me that there was one last lead to follow up. I'd overheard the captain mention a 'late change'. Presumably she meant to our schedule. Were we still following the route Armfield had traced on the nautical chart? With Amelia's help, I double-checked.

During the early part of the afternoon, we seemed to stay more or less on course. As the daylight waned, however, it seemed that our route diverged from his projection: only by a few degrees, but instead of heading straight back to Hammerfest on a south-by-south-easterly course, the *Polar Flow* was veering ever so slightly to the west.

If I'd been able to track him down, I'd have asked Armfield about this as well as everything else, but though I made more circuits of the ship and kept checking my phone there was no sign of him that afternoon . . . at all.

Six o'clock came and went.

There were now just a handful of hours left before the shockwave event, and not many more before we were due back in port.

Mum hadn't replied to me. Neither had Armfield. Though Xander mined the seam of the dark web tirelessly right into the evening, he found nothing new. I felt powerless, rudderless, and horribly becalmed. I knew it was the sort of calm that comes before a storm.

## 53.

I didn't dare hope that Armfield would show up at dinner, and I wasn't disappointed. I waited twenty minutes but I didn't eat: I'd lost my appetite. As soon as it seemed certain he wasn't coming, the three of us returned to our cabin, but not before I'd suffered another of Macmillan's facetious salutes. I swear he mouthed 'Not long now!' at me as we headed past him.

For an agonising hour, which turned into an hour and a half, two, three, I could think of nothing further to do, except hope that Xander would have a breakthrough. But he didn't. The frustration played on his screen-lit face. He barely moved a muscle, just sat there fixed in concentration. I, on the other hand, couldn't stop pacing up and down the little cabin. Sometimes, for me, movement can jog a new thought. With just half an hour to go before midnight I heard myself ask, 'If we stay on this heading, where do we end up?'

'Nowhere much. The coast, a bit to the west of Hammerfest,' said Xander.

'Why go there?'

'Who says we are? We could tack back to port at any time.'

'By why the deviation? What's between us and the coast?'

Xander pulled up a different map, zoomed in on the blank blue sea, and homed in on a pinprick that, as it grew, acquired a name. He read it out, though we could all see it. 'Goliat. Whatever that is.'

'It's an oilfield,' said Amelia. 'A big one, not far offshore.'

'How near it are we?'

Xander's fingers moved quickly. 'Er, we're pretty much there, if this is right.'

I'd already begun putting on my all-weather gear, and I didn't have to wait long for the others to follow me up to the forward observation deck. We arrived there out of breath. Haloed lights were already apparent up ahead. They shimmered in a cluster above the surface of the sea, still a way off, but close enough to distinguish from land. These lights belonged not to a town, a village, or even a homestead, but to an enormous oil rig in the middle of the sea.

As that became clear to me, the *Polar Flow*'s engines quietened and the boat slowed. We were still a couple of hundred metres from the oil platform, but coming to a stop.

I was watching what was happening through a filter of incomprehension, unable to fathom it. What was that light in the sky to the west, for instance, wafting towards us? Did it have anything to do with the new buzzing noise?

Out of nowhere, a gust of needle-sharp snow blew straight into my face. It felt like a slap and it brought me to my senses. The *Polar Flow* had stopped just short of a rig in the Goliat oilfield, and a helicopter was now approaching. Not directly from the rig: that lay to our south, but the copter was drifting towards us from the west. Why did that matter? I couldn't say, but it did.

'What did Timo say about a helicopter in the conversation I overheard?' I asked.

'"The copter pilot knows to get us out of here pronto",' Amelia replied.

'What does that mean?' I asked. Then, without waiting for an answer, 'Quick, follow me, we may not have much time.'

I wanted to get close to the helipad, and I knew just the spot to head for; by now I was as adept at threading my way fore and aft as if I'd been born on board. In under a minute the three of us were crouching on the crane deck at the boat's stern. From here, in the shadow of the control panel, I could see across the helideck to the entrance beyond it. Two figures had moved into the light there.

The nearest, his Norwegian fisherman's sweater clearly visible beneath his open parka, was Macmillan. Behind him Timo's glasses flashed in the light. Both had sizeable rucksacks at their sides. They looked relaxed. Macmillan was leaning casually against the doorframe, craning to see the helicopter's descent. It was close now, all blinking lights and whirring blades, and the pressure from its downdraught was building. Amelia and Xander and I crouched against the bulwark for shelter.

'Where are they headed, do you think?' asked Xander.

'A meeting on the rig, possibly,' said Amelia.

'That doesn't stack up,' I said.

'Why not?'

'Those are expedition rucksacks,' I said, the thought only occurring to me as I articulated it. 'They're leaving for good.'

Armfield was missing. Why? He hadn't replied to my message. Again, why? The snippets of conversation I'd overheard zipped through my head again: What did 'wreckage' refer to? Ditto: 'he'll be in it to take the blame?' What was Timo talking about when he said 'Yes, that will hold?' And how was that 'kinda ironic', according to Macmillan? I thought of the blueprints. The phrase 'right under his nose' followed on its heels. Macmillan's team had loaded all manner of equipment onto the *Polar Flow*. What had they been doing in the forward storage hold? What had made us change course? Why were we drifting slowly toward an oil rig in the dark, beneath the blinking lights of a nimble helicopter, which would shortly touch down?

I couldn't answer any of those questions, not definitively. But their likely answers, taken together, suddenly made horrible sense to me. An act of sabotage was about to take place. I could sense it. When I shut my eyes, I saw a geyser of oil spewing into the sea. That's what the shockwave would do: deliberately trigger an environmental catastrophe, disrupt oil production, and drive up other energy prices. I didn't think this though; I just knew it. And I knew what I had to do to stop it.

I turned the lever on the panel next to me – the one I'd seen the crane guy twist to let out cable when he'd launched the submersible. The drum above us immediately started to

260

spin and the cable, unreeling from it, dropped a metal clasp to the deck a few metres from us. The helicopter sounded cacophonous above us. It was metres from the helipad. I kept the lever pressed down: more cable unspooled in snaking loops at our feet.

Meanwhile, Macmillan and Timo had emerged on the helideck. They were, understandably, focused entirely on the helicopter, and – although they didn't need to – instinctively crouched before its whirring blades. I picked up the clasp. It was like a heavy-duty carabiner, a chunk of metal in the shape of a sprung, snap-lock hook. I was praying for the helicopter to land facing the right way. The slashed-up air beat about our heads: my ears filled with rotor whump and engine whine. These physical sensations pushed me on: I had one chance, a long shot, I knew. I steeled myself to take it.

## 54.

The helicopter touched down gently, its tail pointed our way. Later I learned what type of machine it was: a Bell 429, manned by one pilot and capable of carrying up to seven passengers.

There were only two booked aboard today, and – perhaps because one of them was Finn Macmillan, for whom keeping cool was a religion – they didn't look to be in any hurry to take their seats.

Still, even for Macmillan, boarding an idling helicopter whose blades were still whirring was distracting. He slunk from across the helideck, his pack on one shoulder, his gaze fixed on the open passenger door. Timo, crouching even lower, crabbed along after him. I'm assuming the pilot watched their approach.

That was what I was banking on, at least. As they made their way to the waiting helicopter, I took the clasp and made sure that as much as possible of the unspooled cable was free behind me. Amelia, hands on hips beside me, shouted, 'What are you thinking?' but Xander clearly understood how important it was that the cable didn't snag on anything when I made my dash for it. He was ready to pay it out. Amelia mouthed, 'Oh, I see.'

As Timo followed Macmillan into the passenger cabin, I leaped from the crane deck to the helideck in one adrenalin-fuelled movement. I'd removed my gloves. My left hand clutched a coil of cable; my right held the cold metal clasp. Though the metal was freezing, I was too amped to feel it.

Dragging the cable, which Xander and Amelia paid out behind me as I shot forward, I ran, bent double, in the shadow of the helicopter, right under its tail. The downdraught intensified as I went: the pilot was already throttling up to lift off. Realising this, I took my chance and hurled the clasp with all my strength, simultaneously letting go of the cable, aiming for the gap between the helicopter's left-hand skid and its underbelly.

Mercifully, there was enough slack in the line for the clasp to reach its target: it soared through the gap and bounced down onto the crossbar of the painted H, right beneath the helicopter, just as it lifted off. I dived headlong after it, both hands extended, like a goalkeeper at full stretch. The helicopter was deafening above me, the downdraught a waterfall of noise, but I had hold of the clasp and all I had to do was slam its sprung jaw back onto the cable beneath the skid. Thanks to Amelia and Xander, who'd furiously paid out many more metres of cable from the crane drum, I managed this just in time. As soon as I felt the *click* of the sprung hook-lock biting down on itself I leaped back and vaulted the rail to the lower deck, crashing into it.

'Quick, here!' I screamed. Although they couldn't possibly have heard me, Amelia and Xander already understood what to do. They pressed themselves with me against the bulwark next to the crane's control panel. This was the nearest shelter. Whatever happened to the helicopter, we'd need to protect ourselves from it as best we could. Though I knew I should keep out of sight, I couldn't help looking over the bulwark to see what I'd done.

The helicopter rose three, six, nine metres from the helideck. The crane cable jerked taut. Since it was attached to just one skid, this movement, which the pilot could not have anticipated, yanked the helicopter down and to the left, disrupting its smooth ascent. I'd hoped the pilot would simply land, preventing Macmillan and Timo from escaping. But the cable snagged the skid so harshly that it canted the helicopter over. The rotor blades smashed into the *Polar Flow*'s upper viewing deck. There was an almighty bang, a sheet of orange sparks flared across the ship, and the helicopter slammed into the helideck just metres away. The skid crumpled. The helicopter, driven by the momentum in its blades, careened to one side of the boat. For a horrible second I thought it might plummet overboard or burst into flames. Mercifully, it came to a grinding halt against the rail. Its blades had stopped; now its engine did too. Lights came on all over the *Polar Flow*. An alarm sounded.

## 55.

Members of the *Polar Flow*'s crew sprang into action, swarming onto the deck with fire extinguishers and medical kits and tools. One guy had an angle grinder, another had a crowbar, a third had some sort of jack. They set to work. Timo and Macmillan were going nowhere for now.

It was a quarter to midnight. If I was right about what was going to happen, I had just minutes left to stop it.

'Watch the helicopter,' I said to Xander, holding up my phone. 'If Macmillan goes anywhere, let me know.'

To Amelia I said, 'Come with me.'

We skirted the confusion on the helideck, ducked back inside the ship, and jogged from stern to prow, heading for the storeroom in the ship's bow. Somehow, I had to get that door open. Although I looked on the way, I couldn't find anything heavy with which to attack the lock: everything sizeable we passed – all the chairs, for example – were of course bolted down. There were other storerooms nearby, however, and one housed jet skis and stand-up paddleboards.

265

I grabbed an oar – the best thing I could find, but woefully light – from the rack and ran the last metres to the forward storeroom.

'Armfield!' I bellowed.

There was no answer.

'Jonny!' I shouted.

Was I imagining it, or had there been a muffled response?

I motioned for Amelia to stand back and braced myself to attack the door with the paddle, but she put a hand on my arm to stop me.

'Er, what about that?' she said, nodding at the lock.

'I don't know the combination.'

'But the numbers written in Armfield's notes . . . you've tried those, surely?'

'Which ones?'

Amelia tapped *24000804SWDE* into the keypad and turned the lock handle. It opened. She smiled at me. 'No imagination, crooks.'

I barged past her into the dimly lit hold and was aghast at what I saw. Armfield, stripped to the waist, barefoot, lay on his side among a jumble of plastic boxes, canisters and cables. His ankles and wrists were bound with duct tape. Half his face was obscured by the stuff too: they'd wrapped it around his head many times. He'd rubbed his wrists raw struggling against the tape.

I ran to him. Amelia followed. In silence, we worked to free him. Blood ran down his forearms: his feet were slick with it. How he'd managed to keep breathing, I don't know – the tape covered his nose as well as his mouth. Whoever had done this could have killed him. They'd used multiple lengths of tape. We had nothing to cut it with so had to unwind it instead. Every so often the end disappeared and we had to unpick a new starting point. He lay utterly still as we worked. I was grateful for Amelia's help: her fingers were nimbler than mine. I worked on the tape covering his face while she unbound his hands and feet. Amelia finished first, then took over from me. My hands were shaking with rage and fear and love.

When, finally, the last of the tape came free of Armfield's mouth, he rolled to all fours and coughed and spat, muttering, 'Thank you.' Galvanising himself, he said it again, more firmly. 'Thank you.' Then he looked at me. 'Where are they?'

I explained what had happened.

'The device is in that crate,' he said. 'They drugged me, carried me down here, tied me up. I can't believe I was so –'

'We have eight minutes,' I said, taking off my coat and handing it to him. He accepted the offer, leaped to his bare feet and, though he must have been in excruciating pain, he managed to limp/stride/jog to his cabin. He'd stowed a safe-box under his bed. Retrieving it, he held his thumbs against sensors in the handles. When they registered his prints, the metal lid snapped open. It looked like the box held a chunky laptop, but when he flipped it open, he revealed a foam cut-out plugged with metal components. I'm still amazed that his fingers, so recently purple and incapacitated by the tape, worked with their customary efficiency, but a combination of simple muscle memory and Armfield's ability to endure pain meant he had the handgun assembled, loaded and cocked in under thirty seconds.

With less than five minutes before the midnight deadline, Armfield barged his way through the *Polar Flow*'s crew, who surrounded the stricken helicopter, to find Macmillan – looking far from cool now – remonstrating with one of the *Polar Flow*'s medically trained crew.

'Get off me!' I heard him yell. 'I need to – you don't understand!'

'No, but I do,' said Armfield, sliding past the medic. I noticed that Armfield was still barefoot, standing on a deck of frozen metal, but the real coldness was in his voice. 'Come with me,' he hissed, putting the gun to Macmillan's head. 'Everyone else, for your own good, back off.'

The medic put his hands in the air and stood to one side.

Holding Macmillan by the scruff of the neck, and with the muzzle of his pistol buried behind his ear, Armfield marched the American back the way we'd come. He didn't rush, or berate him, or say anything at all until we – Xander included – arrived at the forward hold, the door to which was still ajar. Through it we went. Armfield took three brisk steps inside then kicked Macmillan behind the left knee, dropping him to the ground in front of the crate he'd pointed out earlier.

'Time?' he asked.

Amelia held her phone up to me.

'We have seventy seconds,' I said.

Armfield lowered the gun to his side. It was unnecessary now. Utterly calmly he addressed Macmillan. 'Disarm it now, or we all die.'

# 56.

'No plan is perfect,' Armfield said.

Macmillan had been thorough, but he must have known all along that the whole thing hinged on his being able to jump ship when the time came. With Armfield neutralised, he must mostly have been worried about the weather. It turned out that we were the bigger threat. As soon as the helicopter came down and he realised he was stuck on board, he knew that his only hope lay in disabling the device he'd planted in the *Polar Flow*'s prow. Even if he'd managed to lower one of the boat's launches, he and Timo would not, in the time they had left, have been able to get far enough away in it to be safe. That's why he'd been struggling with the medic in the helicopter. In a way, he was grateful for Armfield's intervention. He didn't want to die: he simply wanted to pull off a deal that would make him – even more – spectacularly rich.

And damn the consequences.

Dead crew, dead Armfield, dead kids: so what?

Dead oil rig, dead rig hands, ruptured pipelines: so what?

Catastrophic oil spill in the Barents Sea, neatly timed to increase the value of investments in liquid natural gas and other sources of power in the region (renewable, whatever): so what?!

So a lot, it turned out.

Faced with the ultimate consequence, Macmillan was more frightened than furious. He and whimpering Timo, marched forward by the seething helicopter pilot, came straight to the forward hold. On arrival Macmillan promptly opened the crate and keyed in the digits to disable the device, with seconds to spare. Watching him do it, Amelia admitted she wouldn't have guessed at that particular code: she'd got lucky with the one on the door. 'Understandably,' she said, 'they put more thought into the sequence that armed and disarmed the weapon.'

Once he was satisfied that Macmillan had neutralised the threat, Armfield used the same roll of duct tape that Macmillan and Timo had bound him with to tie up the pair. For good measure, Captain Lander placed them under armed watch. After she had been satisfied that Armfield's explanation of events was true, and with the wreck of the helicopter lashed securely to the deck, she set a course back to Hammerfest, just a few hours south.

Later, when I was alone with Armfield in his cabin, he repeated, 'No plan is perfect' then went on to elaborate. 'Mine wasn't, for sure. I was banking on them not knowing. But something I did must have made Macmillan suspicious of me, and once he'd worked out that I knew what they were really up to he decided to make it look like the whole sabotage element of the deal was my doing. I doubt an investigator would have been taken in by it, but either way, with the *Polar Flow* at the bottom of the sea, polluted by the oil spill, Macmillan would have bought himself time to cover up his involvement.'

'I see,' I murmured.

'The failure was mine. I was preoccupied.'

He'd boiled a kettle when we entered his room, and now spooned coffee into two mugs and filled them with steaming water. Without asking if I wanted milk or sugar (I didn't), he handed me a mug. 'You were part of my plan too, obviously.'

'How?' I asked.

'Haven't you guessed?'

Though it wasn't an answer, I replied with: 'We've had a lot to work out.'

'True,' he said, rubbing his wrists. 'Well, I knew what you were up to from the outset. I appreciate that you were serious about making your film. But you were also testing me, right?'

I lowered my gaze.

'It's OK. I'd have done the same in your place. In fact, I did. I wanted to give you a chance to make the best possible film, with the trek and so on, but I was testing you at the same time.'

I looked back up at him. His expression reminded me of myself.

'Don't hate me for it, but the stunt with Kotler, for example – that was part of the test. I wanted to see how resilient you – and your good friends – would be under that sort of pressure. He's fine, by the way. Sends his best wishes.'

I bit my lip. 'I thought he was dead.'

'I know. Yet you didn't panic. On the contrary, you did everything right. Attempting a rescue. Staying safe on the ice. Taking down the coordinates. Finishing the journey alone. Contacting me. Rendezvousing with Lukas. All of it, you did well. Even handling the completely unexpected: wolves attacking Tikaani's dogs, for example. That wasn't in the script, but you coped. Caleb, in particular, showed extraordinary fortitude there. You should know that he's on the mend.'

'I'm glad,' I said, meaning it.

'And all the while, behind the scenes, you – largely thanks to Xander – were making huge inroads into uncovering what was really going on with GreenSword Investments. I left you a few clues: the folder, for example, but you were piecing stuff together pretty well without them. Deleting the film footage of the meeting: that was another obstacle/clue I put in your way. I thought that eventually you'd confront me and I'd be able to tell you the truth. I never imagined I'd be so distracted by your progress – and proud, I admit it, proud – that I'd take my eye off the ball long enough for those greedy maniacs to get one over on me. I was convinced I'd fooled them. All it took was a stop-a-rhino dose of sedative and they had me neutralised.'

'You'd have found a way . . .' I began, but tailed off.

'No. I wouldn't. If you hadn't been here, none of us would be here now.' He shrugged and said simply, 'I am for ever in your debt.'

I recognised something strange in that moment, a glint in his eye I'd only ever seen before in one person: Mum. She'd looked at me like that the first time I beat her at chess. Mum's not a bad player herself, and never once threw a game when I was learning. The first time I beat her was fair and square, and I could tell she was annoyed. She's competitive, like me. But her disappointment in herself then, though real, was outweighed by her delight: her son had won! Armfield was looking at me now with the same mix of regret – he'd let his guard down with Macmillan – and pleasure. I – his son, Jack – had been there to help him.

'No plan is perfect,' he whispered again. 'You have to be able to improvise. This wasn't how I wanted to convince you I'm for real. But I am. You see that now.'

'I do,' I said. And I did. And it felt good. For some reason I smelled bacon and eggs and saw him sitting at the kitchen table on a Sunday morning reading the newspaper while Mum tapped something into her iPad, three cups of coffee, black and strong and hot, on the zinc-topped table between us.

'But the test,' I said. 'What was it for? You know you're my father. I was the one who needed convincing.'

'I wanted to see what you were made of,' he said. 'You, Amelia and Xander. After Somalia, I suspected I knew, and now I do for sure. You're growing up fast, but you're still young, and believe it or not that makes you uniquely capable. Here, for example, you foiled a plot partly because the perpetrator wasn't cautious enough around you. They underestimated you. I explained in London what I do.

In Somalia I was shutting down child-soldiering camps; here I was deployed to avert an ecological catastrophe. My work is endless, difficult and often dangerous. It requires a resilience and a resourcefulness – and you've proven you have those skills. This isn't a job offer, just an invitation to . . . stay involved. All four of you: Caleb proved himself too.' He took a deep swig of his coffee. 'Think about it.'

'I will,' I said, and sipped from my own mug. It was scalding, and tasted exactly right.

# Epilogue

Our film did not win the On the Brink competition. The one that did was nowhere near as good, but it had two features the judges particularly liked. The first was an informative voiceover done by a man who sounded like David Attenborough. The second – you guessed it – was a sequence about polar bears. The judges thought our polar-bear-free entry was a bit too focused on adventure at the expense of the landscape under threat. Whatever. They liked it enough to give it a 'highly commended'.

Mum thought we were robbed. At the awards ceremony – held in the Natural History Museum, no less – she was all for giving the judges a talking-to after they made their announcements. Jonny (I still find it hard to call him Dad) had to hold her back. She was kidding, of course, but there's truth in every joke, and she's not the first mum in history to put their child first.

I'd wanted to splice the story of GreenSword's criminality into the film, but for all sorts of reasons – mostly to do with confidentiality and expensive lawyers – we weren't able to do that. It's been frustrating, but Jonny isn't interested in pressing charges against Macmillan; that would just bring unwanted publicity. Since the shockwave disruption event never happened, they didn't have a chance to make any money from it, so they can't be done for that either. And the owners of the *Polar Flow* were, apparently, easily bought off. Where the EWS/DEW device ended up, I have no idea: Jonny took care of that. Although Jonny assures me that Macmillan, Timo and the others will face the music eventually, I bet the money they have at their disposal will delay whatever those consequences turn out to be.

So it goes.

The scene that flashed before me – of me, Mum and Jonny at the kitchen table on a Sunday morning – hasn't, of course, materialised. The two of them go way back, but they didn't work out as a couple for a reason. Although Mum wasn't keen to elaborate, she did say that whatever they shared hasn't entirely gone away. For their sake as well as my own, I'm still hopeful.

Meanwhile, Amelia, Caleb, Xander and I have talked about Jonny's proposal. They're interested in hearing more about it, of course. What exactly would we do for him? How would it work? When you've been through the sort of stuff we have together, you need more of the same – or at least something similar – to get through the boredom of everyday life.

Sure, school can be a challenge and there are always more jumps to hit and trails to ride, but we've been lucky enough to see some of the world – good and bad – and it's just made me want to see more.

I've set up a meeting for the four of us next week. Because the painting means something to me now, we're gathering in front of Whistlejacket in the National Gallery. Jonny texted back *good choice* when I suggested the venue, and Amelia messaged us all with the story of how the artist had planned to paint in a backdrop and rider, but was persuaded to let the horse stand alone. It was nice to know something before she did for once. I messaged back immediately, telling her that the original horse had been so unnerved by the painting that it had attempted to attack its own portrait.

*Makes you think*, texted Xander, adding, *What's the agenda for this meeting then?*

I replied: *No agenda. I've just put it in my diary under The Next Adventure.*

Wilbur Smith is an international bestselling author, having sold over 130 million copies of his incredible adventure novels. His Courtney family saga is the longest running series in publishing history, and with the Jack Courtney Adventures he brings the series to a new generation.

Chris Wakling read his first Wilbur Smith book when he was Jack's age: fourteen. He writes novels and travel journalism, and is available for events and interviews.

For all the latest information about Wilbur, visit:
www.wilbursmithbooks.com
facebook.com/WilburSmith
www.wilbur-niso-smithfoundation.org

Wilbur Smith donates twenty per cent of profits received from the sale of this copy to The Wilbur & Niso Smith Foundation. The Foundation's focus is to encourage adventure writing and literacy and find new talent.

For more information, please visit
www.wilbur-niso-smithfoundation.org

# Piccadilly
**P R E S S**

Thank you for choosing a Piccadilly Press book.

If you would like to know more about our
authors, our books or if you'd just like to know
what we're up to, you can find us online.

## www.piccadillypress.co.uk

And you can also find us on:

## We hope to see you soon!